Stories Not from the Bible

Robbie Mahair

© 2019 Michael Robert Mahair II

All rights reserved. This book or any portion thereof may not be reproduced or used in any manner whatsoever without the express written permission of the publisher except for the use of brief quotations in a book review.

Printed in the United States of America.
First Printing, 2019
First Edition

ISBN-13: 978-1-949495-03-4

This is a work of fiction. Names, characters, businesses, places, events and incidents are either the products of the author's imagination or used in a fictitious manner.

http://robbiemahair.com

Edited by Hannah Donor
hleedonor@gmail.com

Book Cover Design by ebooklaunch.com

Introduction

Introductions tend to be boring, right? I get that. So, if you want to skip this and jump straight into the first story, please feel free to. But for any who continue, I'll do my best to keep this short.

This book was born out of Bible study.

Years ago, I was introduced to the concept of an "Inductive Bible Study" and immediately fell in love with it. Inductive Bible Study is a fancy name for a fairly simple concept: taking a passage from the Bible, first you read it and try to figure out what it says; second, using the words of the passage, you try to figure out what main points the author is trying to get across; and third, you figure out how those main points apply to you. These three steps are typically expressed as: "Observe, Interpret, Apply."

Again, it sounds simple, but it's surprisingly hard to do well. Our natural implication is to take what we already believe and allow it to color whatever it is that we are reading. It takes a bit of discipline to force yourself to see what the author is actually saying rather than what resonates with you. For this reason, it's often helpful to do this Bible study with a group of people who can keep each other accountable by gently (or, sometimes, not so gently) pointing out when one among them is drawing a conclusion about a passage that simply isn't justified by the author's actual words.

One of the elements of this type of Bible study is the concept of "putting yourself in the story." What would it be like if you were one of the Pharisees whom Jesus accused of being a child of Satan? How was King Darius feeling when he realized that he'd been tricked into condemning his most trusted ruler, Daniel, to death in the lion's den? What must Balaam have been thinking when his donkey suddenly started talking to him? This type of exercise is tremendously beneficial. It is easy to think of those in the Bible as simply "characters": far-off, fictional villains or heroes going through other-worldly challenges that bear no resemblance to our lives. Putting yourself in the story forces you to see those in the Bible as they are: real people, who are just as normal as you and me. It allows you to really understand what's happening, why the people are doing what they are doing, what the full implications of that event or teaching are, and so on.

But here's another thing about putting yourself in the story: it's also a lot of fun! Considering what Balaam must have been thinking when his donkey started talking to him makes me chuckle, but considering what *the donkey* must have been thinking when it suddenly gained enough intelligence to have a conversation with a human *really* entertains me. Did that donkey have just enough time to ponder the implications of his new intellect and how fleeting it was before it was taken away from him? Or maybe he even wished it *would* be taken away from him, and that he could go back to a simpler life where his only concern was his next meal. Or perhaps the donkey was always intelligent, the only intelligent donkey that has ever existed, but he was smart enough not to talk in front of humans lest it bring problems on himself. Did he practice speaking in the barn when no one was watching? When he was annoyed with his master, did he play pranks on him, knowing the master would never suspect the donkey? I don't know exactly how this worked, but every possibility I can think of entertains and fascinates me.

The Bible is filled with stories just like this, yet since the original books of the Bible and every copy were written painstakingly by hand, no ink was wasted, and therefore many fascinating stories get summed up in a mere few sentences. Details of tremendous significance are difficult to catch unless the reader is paying close attention.

And that is why I created this book of Stories (Not) from the Bible. I wanted to highlight these details that are easy to miss and to explore some of these characters and stories that we only get a brief glimpse of. Many of the events, details, and even characters are entirely fictional and a product of my own imagination. But wherever something comes directly from the Bible, I have added a reference to the chapters and verses so that you can go and explore these stories for yourself. I have used the words of the Bible as my anchors, setting them in stone, but the space between the stones is where I play.

I hope you enjoy these stories, and I hope in at least a small way they increase your love for the Bible and the one who inspired it.

Contents

Good Shepherd	1
The Other Daughter	21
Bold	48
Golgotha	59
Faithful	78
The Unlikely Angel	91
Saul's Fall: How Four Men Changed the World	107
Twelve Coats	130
The Victorious Son of the Baggage King	143
The Jailer	165

Good Shepherd

The eight[1] sons of Jesse sat at the dinner table. Each one was more impressive than the last, unless of course you went the wrong way, in which case at the end of the wrong way you would find David. He was a handsome boy whose dark skin suggested he was no stranger to laboring in the sun and whose dark eyes suggested that his thoughts were just as busy as his hands. But he was no comparison to his brothers.

Anyway, everyone knows you aren't supposed to go the wrong way, otherwise they wouldn't call it the wrong way. And in this case, if you tried, you probably wouldn't get to David or to any of Jesse's other sons, because there, to the right of the head of the table, you would find Eliab.[2] Once you had seen Eliab, you certainly wouldn't be paying much attention to anyone else.

Eliab: the first son of Jesse. He was nearly as tall as King Saul himself. He was as strong as an ox. He was a powerful warrior who had proven himself in battle time and again. He had a face that looked as if it had been carved by a woman with the hands of a master sculptor and the hormones of a thirteen-year-old.[3]

Jesse sat down at the head of the table, unabashedly beaming with pride at the sight of all of his gathered sons. Despite his age his strength had not left him. It wasn't often these days that they were all able to eat at one table. His three oldest served in the king's army[4] and spent much time away on campaigns. But here and now they were all together, and Jesse couldn't be happier. The face of his wife, sitting to his left, reflected his pride.

As they began their meal, Eliab spoke. "Father, I was at the city gate today, and I heard some interesting news. They say Samuel is coming."[5] The word "Samuel" was presented with great care, as if he

---

[1] 1 Samuel 17:12
[2] 1 Samuel 17:13
[3] 1 Samuel 16:6-7
[4] 1 Samuel 17:13-14
[5] 1 Samuel 16:1

was afraid of dropping it.

"Samuel?" asked Jesse. "He's coming here? To Bethlehem?"

"Yes. Very soon, I'm told."

"Samuel?" asked David, excitedly. "The prophet of Yahweh? The one God *himself* talks to?"

Eliab shot a cold glare toward David. "Yes, David. The prophet. Did you think I was talking about some *other* Samuel? Samuel the shepherd, maybe?"

David opened his mouth to protest and looked around the table at the rest of his brothers for some sort of support, but, as per the fate of youngest siblings everywhere, his silent plea was met only with mocking smiles. So, his eyes sought solace in the face of his father, but Jesse appeared lost in thought.

"Samuel," said Jesse. "Samuel. This is not good."[6]

"They say King Saul is not pleased with him," offered up Abinadab,[7] the second oldest. "There are rumors among the other soldiers that he wants him dead."[8]

Eliab burst out into laughter. "Dead? Oh, brother, he would not do that. You should have seen him at Gilgal, after we crushed that worthless King Agag"—the name was nearly spit out of Eliab's mouth—"and the rest of the Amalekites. Saul was practically groveling before Samuel.[9] He's afraid of him. Only God knows why someone like Saul should be afraid of someone like Samuel."

"We all should be," said Jesse.

"Ha! I'm not," said Eliab. "He's just some old man, a relic of a time now past. The time of the judges is over. This is the age of *kings*, Father! King Saul, whatever his faults, is a great man! God has chosen him, and he chose well. By the strength of Saul and his mighty warriors"—it was lost on none at the table that Eliab was among these warriors, but just in case he laid a humble hand on his chest to show that he was included—"we will crush our enemies and expel them from our good land forever. Samuel's time is over. We can put our trust in the

---

[6] 1 Samuel 16:4
[7] 1 Samuel 17:13
[8] 1 Samuel 16:2
[9] 1 Samuel 15:24-31

strength of those God has chosen."

"You sound like Samson,"[10] said David.

Eliab turned on David, his perfect face contorting into the mocking expression he seemed to reserve only for his youngest sibling. But then it softened to a questioning tone, and he replaced the usual scathing response with, "You say that as if it is a bad thing? I could only hope to be as great as Samson. By the strength of his arm thousands of Philistines were destroyed. We are still fighting the Philistines today, and strength like that is what we need to save our people."

David was about to respond that he hadn't intended this as a compliment, but Jesse, seemingly oblivious to the discussion between his sons, continued, "If Samuel is coming here, this could be bad news for all of us. We could all be under some kind of curse."

"Maybe he is bringing us a blessing," said David. "Isn't God good and merciful?"

"I can't imagine what God would want to bless us for," replied Jesse.

For a time, all that could be heard was chewing, as each member of the family was temporarily enveloped in their individual musings about what the arrival of Samuel could mean.

David interrupted the silence. "Dad, tell us the story of Samson and the lion."[11]

Jesse took a moment to stagger out of whatever imaginary scene was playing out in his mind, but then, slowly, his eyes lit up. The only thing a father loves more than telling a story to unsuspecting children is telling a story to eager children. He didn't seem to notice Eliab's rolling eyes, or the various other expressions of mild exasperation on the faces of his sons around the table. Secretly, he absolutely did notice such things. One of the delights of old age is imparting wisdom on youth, even if you have to do it against their will.

"Ah, yes, Samson. He was a Nazarite, you know. Dedicated to God before he was even born. His hair was never to be cut."[12]

"Just like Samuel!"[13] said David. "He's really old though. I bet his

---

[10] Judges 13-16
[11] Judges 14
[12] Judges 13:5, Numbers 6:1-21
[13] 1 Samuel 1:11

hair is really long."

"Yes, just like Samuel!" said Jesse, carefully ignoring the "really old" comment. Jesse had long ago gotten used to men much younger than himself being referred to as "old".

"And he was judge of Israel too, just like Samuel used to be. He was a very different man, though. But … yes, the story of the lion. I was a much younger man when it happened, and at that time everyone in Israel knew that story."

Jesse paused, presumably for dramatic effect, though it was possibly just to annoy the older sons, who had heard this story and many others like it more times than they could count.

"They say Samson was going down to Timnah. A girl there—a beautiful girl, though she was a Philistine—had caught his eye. He had asked his parents to get her for him, because he wanted to marry her. They protested, of course, but he insisted and they finally consented. So, he was going down to Timnah to meet with the family. When he neared the vineyards of Timnah, suddenly a massive lion attacked him! It was the largest lion he'd ever seen! They say it was nearly one thousand pounds!"

A careful observer would have noted the smile on the face of Jesse's wife, accompanied by a laugh that was almost perfectly disguised as a cough. She was also quite old, and also knew this story, and therefore she was well aware that the lion was young and not particularly large. Jesse often said that a little embellishment added spice to a good story.

"He didn't see the lion until it was almost upon him! It leapt out at him, jumping so high its feet were over his head—though he was a tall man, even taller than Eliab here—and just when it had nearly landed on him, and its jaws were opened wide prepared to crush his skull, and all seemed lost …"

He paused again, relishing the expectant look on David's face (and possibly the impatient one on Eliab's). His voice grew quieter, and all ears at the table strained to hear him, though they all knew exactly what he would say next, right down to the minutest intonations.

"Samson was suddenly filled with the Spirit of Yahweh. He reached his arms out. He grabbed the lion by its jaws"—and here his voice rose—"and *ripped* them apart! He did it as if it was nothing. The lion fell dead at his feet. He didn't tell his parents about it at first."

The words "the Spirit of Yahweh" echoed in David's head.

"Then he went on to Timnah and confirmed that he wanted to marry the girl. Later, during his wedding, he used a riddle about the lion to make fools of the Philistines,[14] and when they cheated him, he defeated them all. Killing the lion was his first great act. He was the most powerful warrior Israel has ever seen, and he won many victories over the Philistines. No one could stop him."

"See, David?" said Eliab. "Strength. God used the strength of his servant Samson to defeat the Philistines. Strength!"

"The Spirit of Yahweh," said David.

"What?" asked Eliab, scowling.

"The Spirit of Yahweh. That's what you said, right dad?" David looked into the eyes of his father. "That's what you said. Strength doesn't matter. It doesn't matter how big the lion is. God doesn't lose."

"Boy!" exclaimed Eliab, now making no effort to conceal his contempt. "Use that mouth of yours for eating! Why are you trying to make a fool of your older brothers in front of your father? You are the youngest one here but you try to teach us?"

"What did I do now?"[15] asked David.

"David," said Jesse. It was a single word, but that one word was said in a tone backed up by years of a father's authority. "This is your older brother. You don't talk to him that way. Listen to him and eat quietly."

David, flushed, lowered his eyes and was silent.

"But he's right, you know," continued Jesse, calming almost as quickly as he was aroused. "Samson was a foolish man. God used him to bless his people, but Samson himself did not see any of the blessings. He died young, childless, blind, and humiliated."[16]

Eliab did not respond, but his expression was that of a man unconvinced but unwilling to argue further. He decided to change the subject.

"Speaking of lions," he said, "they also said at the city gate that there have been attacks on flocks in the western fields. Be careful,

---

[14] Judges 14:12-20
[15] 1 Samuel 17:29
[16] Judges 16:23-31

Father, or you may lose some of yours."

Jesse let out a noncommittal grunt in between bites.

An idea seemed to strike Eliab and he stared mischievously at David. There was now a glint in his eye.

"Perhaps," he said, "it would be unwise to leave the flock up to the hired servants? They only care about the money, as you know. They will run at the first sign of trouble."[17]

Jesse looked up from his plate at Eliab and seemed to consider this. His wife did the same, though her reserved facial expression belied a hint of concern. She glanced back and forth from Eliab to David.

"Hmm," said Jesse. "Maybe you're right."

Eliab continued, the glint in his eye now growing so bright it would almost glow in the dark. He looked meaningfully at David. "Weren't you telling me earlier what a talented shepherd young Da—"

"I'll do it!" blurted out David, suddenly. Eliab smiled. His mother looked worried. Jesse just stared thoughtfully.

"I'm sorry for interrupting, Father. Please forgive me. But I will do it! You can count on me. I won't lose any sheep or goat you put in my care!"

Before Jesse could answer, Eliab spoke again. "Marvelous! What a bold brother we have, eh?" He looked around the table at his other brothers, clearly expecting to share a devious smile with them, but even Abinadab, the second oldest, seemed to think he was going too far.

Jesse was unaware of all of this. He was contemplating the hopeful look in his youngest's eyes. "Hmm ... no, I'm sorry David. I can't spare anyone around here. There's too much to do. Onan is already out there. I can't send you, too."

"Then let me do it alone, Father! I'll send Onan back to you. I'm ready! You've taught me how to be a good shepherd. Let me show you what I can do!"

After a long stare peppered with a few chewing motions, Jesse finally nodded reluctantly and said, "Okay, son. I'm counting on you. You leave first thing tomorrow."

---

[17] John 10:12-13

"Thanks, Dad! This is great! I won't let you down, you'll see! I won't lose a single one in my care! Not one! I've got to go get my things ready! I need to pack my lyre.[18] I can practice while I'm out there. This'll be great!"

As David rapidly shoveled the last morsels of his food into his mouth, Eliab said, "Perhaps you can lull the lions to sleep with one of those boring songs?"

His brothers chuckled.

Jesse looked thoughtful. "David, don't run off just yet. I have something for you."

Soon his old body was on its feet ambling rapidly—a movement which should, by rights, be impossible, but somehow old men are capable of it. As he left the room he was smiling excitedly. When he returned, in his hand was a long, sturdy-looking piece of wood with a crook on one end.

"It's a staff," he said. "A proper shepherd's staff, just for you. It's the best one I've ever made. I've been waiting until you were ready to give it to you, and I think that's now."

David, wide-eyed and swallowing the last bite of food, got up and walked over to his father. With great care, he took the staff from his father. He turned it over and over and ran his hands along the wood.

"It's ... fantastic, Father! Maybe my lyre's no help against a lion, but this ..."

Eliab laughed. "Is a lion like a dog, David, that you would come at it with a stick?"[19]

Jesse turned to his eldest. "Hey! That's a good stick!"

He turned back to David. "Now, run along and prepare your things."

David bolted out of the room, causing another round of laughter among his brothers.

~

David was up early the next morning and, after a short and

---

[18] 1 Samuel 16:18
[19] 1 Samuel 17:43

thoroughly unnecessary lecture from his father about which land was yet to be grazed and many reminders to take it easy on the young lambs, he was out making the short trek to the western fields where the sheep and goats were currently grazing.

It was an easy journey. On the way he admired his new staff, and a few times he practiced using it as a walking stick. Being a very young man, he wasn't entirely sure what, exactly, the use of a walking stick was, but the older shepherds used it that way and he thought they probably had a good reason for it, so he might as well start now.

As he passed the only stream along his journey, he stopped briefly. He examined the smooth stones in the river, selected a few that were to his liking, and put them in his shepherd's bag before moving on.[20]

As David approached the field, he saw the hired servant, Onan, walking back up a hill to the rest of the sheep and goats. Onan was carrying Nabal, and for this David immediately felt sorry for him. But, right on the heels of feeling sorry for the older man, he realized that soon he would be the one dealing with Nabal, and then he decided he'd feel sorry for himself instead.

Nabal was ... well, she was Nabal. Her name meant "Fool,"[21] and it was well-earned. She was a plump little ewe who was much too curious for her own good.

Undoubtedly, Onan was carrying her back after rescuing her from whatever hole she'd fallen into, or thicket she'd managed to get stuck in, or maybe just field that she'd decided to stand in the middle of, all by herself, for no apparent reason.

To be fair, the rest of the sheep were just as likely to get stuck somewhere, but they'd at least have the good sense to do it together. David swore if that little ewe could write, she'd decide it would be terribly fashionable to walk around with a sign that said: "Free Mutton."

Even so, David had to admit that Nabal had a special place in his heart. Individuality is not a common trait among sheep and, foolish or not, David couldn't help but find it endearing.

As David drew close enough to talk to Onan, he hid the new staff

---

[20] 1 Samuel 17:40
[21] 1 Samuel 25:25

behind his back.

"Onan!"

"David? What are you doing out here, Young Master?" The older man turned with a genuine smile on his face—the kind he reserved for David; the kind that accentuated the wrinkles framing his eyes; the kind David's brothers never received.

Nabal, sitting atop Onan's shoulders, said, "Baaa." It was her friendly "Baaa", the one she used when she either was greeting someone she knew or asking for a scratch behind the ear or, more likely, both.

"Dad sent me. He wants me to watch the flock for a few days," David paused for effect, a little trick he'd learned from his father's storytelling, "by myself!"

"Baaa," said Nabal, who was still waiting not-so-patiently for that scratch behind the ear.

"Oh, ho, look at you, Young Master!" said Onan. "A proper shepherd then now, eh?"

"Yup," said David. "I've even got ... this!" He swung the staff around from behind his back and held it up proudly.

Onan moved closer, with Nabal still on his back, and inspected the staff with enthusiasm.

"Baaa," said Nabal, who seemed not the least bit impressed with this big piece of wood and, in fact, was rather unhappy that it was occupying hands that could otherwise be used for scratching her head.

"Oh my, Master. That's very nice. Very nice, indeed. I suppose you won't be needing to borrow mine anymore, then? Well, I wouldn't either. It's a rickety old thing, compared to that beauty in your hands."

Onan moved closer still, now almost conspiratorially. His voice became low and took on the informal tone he only dared to use when he was sure no one was around but David. "You've earned this, you have. I'm proud of you, my boy."

David beamed.

"Baaa," said Nabal, and nudged her head closer to David. She finally got her scratch.

The two—or three, if shoulder-perched sheep are to be taken into account—turned to continue up the hill to the rest of the flock.

"So," said Onan, in that tone with the familiar mix of joviality and sarcasm that has been used by men working together since time immemorial, "does this mean I get a few days off?"

"Oh, of course," said David, sarcastically. "As you know, Eliab's in town. And as usual he's taking it upon himself to help out dad by ... managing ... the servants. I'm sure once you head back and report to Eliab, he'll tell you to just relax and take it easy for a few days. He'll probably have you sit down for supper and serve you wine, just to show how appreciative he is."

Onan laughed and said, "Ah, don't you worry. I can handle him. I'd rather work for your household than any other I've seen, that's for sure, Eliab or no."

He stopped, and David stopped in response. A ponderous look crept onto Onan's face.

Nabal said "Baaa" again, just on general principle.

Onan continued, "There's something about your father. Something about you. I mean, sure, you're all tall, fine, handsome men. But there's something more. Eight sons, my master has. Eight. And God has blessed all of you. Even us servants remain healthy and strong. Your flocks prosper. Their young live. None of you children have been lost to disease or death, even though your older brothers are men of war."

He paused again. He looked meaningfully at David.

"Yahweh is watching over you. I wouldn't want to be anywhere else."

David didn't know how to respond to this. A few uncomfortable seconds passed. They felt like an eternity to him. But then Onan mercifully turned and continued the short trek up the hill.

"Baaa," said Nabal, only this time it meant, "Put me down." Onan obliged. She trotted over to be with the rest of the flock.

It was a pleasant summer mid-morning. A light breeze offset the heat, which was never too bad to begin with in the pleasant hill country of Bethlehem.

The sheep and the goats grazed together quite peacefully. The time of year meant that the lambs and kids were strong enough to keep pace with the rest of the animals. They could be seen darting here and there among the flock, alternating between eating, playing, and attempting to annoy the nearest adult they could find.

Onan and David spent some time watching the flock together, under the shared guise of Onan getting David up to speed on the current state of the sheep and goats. They both knew this wasn't the real reason. Onan had found that a bit of mental preparation was always a good idea when he would soon have to work for Eliab, so he wasn't too keen on heading back immediately. David was happy for his company, even if only for a little while.

As they chatted, David carefully avoided the subject of the recent lion attacks. He wasn't sure if Onan had heard about them, and he feared his reaction. Would he try to convince Jesse to let him stay in the fields with David? Would he be offended that his father didn't trust him, though he'd been a loyal servant for as long as David could remember?

After about an hour they knew they could delay no longer, and Onan finally started the short walk back home.

As he watched Onan leave, excitement welled within David. This was it! He was a shepherd, a proper shepherd, watching the flock all by himself!

When Onan was out of sight he took another look at his cherished staff, and then did an excited little dance, the kind that would surely illicit condescending remarks from other humans but didn't seem to bother the sheep in the least.

Then he went about his work.

As the sheep grazed, he did what he always did, except this time he did it without the help and guidance of Onan or one of his brothers. His eyes and ears were vigilant, always searching for signs of predators. He scratched the head of any sheep or goat that came up looking for a little attention. He kept the flock moving from one field to the next as necessary. At mid-day, he brought them down to the stream to drink from the cool water and lounge in the shade of the trees, where he again spent a couple of minutes searching for smooth stones to his liking, which he placed in his bag alongside the ones he'd collected earlier. In the latter part of the day, he led them back up the hills again.

Many times, he had to stop to collect a sheep or goat that was heading off track or managed to get stuck somewhere. Nabal was in particularly fine form that day, making various excursions from the rest of the flock in a very individualistic and unsheeplike manner. She even managed to get stuck in the exact same hole both on the way to and from the stream.

Like most shepherds, David found he needed hobbies for the long periods where there simply wasn't much else to do. It was more than just for fun. Boredom meant a lack of diligence, and a lack of diligence meant you lost animals.

David's main hobby was his lyre. Throughout the day he practiced. He played songs he knew well. He played songs he was currently composing. He played songs that he made up on the spot; cheery little tunes that only the sheep would ever hear. Often, he sang as he played. Anyone around would have complimented him on his skill and clear, pleasant voice, except of course that there wasn't anyone around aside from the sheep and goats, who weren't big on giving compliments.

In the latter part of the day, when he tired of the lyre and still found himself with little to do, he opened up his shepherd bag and pulled out the stones. He took one out, examined it again, and then placed it into his sling. He directed it towards a tree, about 150 feet away, and let fly. It hit its target with a satisfying *thwack* sound, leaving a small indent in the bark.

David took another stone from the bag, loaded it, and loosed it on the tree. Another *thwack*. The indent grew larger.

Again and again he slung the stones, and each one landed in the same spot, without fail. With each impact the dent grew until pieces began flying off and the heartwood was exposed.

At last he retrieved the final stone. He loaded it as well, but then paused. He wondered if he should keep it, in case it would be any help against a lion. Then he wondered if anyone would make fun of him for thinking that a small stone could somehow take down a lion. Then he thought about how silly it was to wonder what other people would think about what he thought, since neither he nor they could know what each other were thinking. Finally, he laughed at himself, which seemed the only appropriate response at this juncture. He flung the final stone at the tree and it hit exactly like all the others.

As afternoon gave way to evening, David found a field with a large rock, which he sat on. Soon he would bring the sheep and goats to a nearby cave to spend the night, but not yet.

This was his favorite part. The end of the day was nearing. A peace and a stillness began to permeate everything. There were no arguments to be heard between his brothers. There was no criticism from Eliab to tolerate. There was no father or mother to please. It was not silent, but the sheep and the wind provided an almost melodious backdrop of sound that was far more pleasant than any silence.

The sheep too seemed peaceful. They were contented to be quietly relaxing under the protection of their shepherd.

David smiled.

And then suddenly there was an image in his mind. It was an image of the true God, Yahweh. David was no longer the shepherd; he was the sheep. Yahweh had provided the sunlight, the breeze, the happy animals, and even the rock to sit on, all for the good and pleasure of his precious little sheep, David. David was contented to sit quietly under Yahweh's protection.

Yahweh smiled.

David picked up his lyre and played a tune. He sang, and it seemed to him that the words came too effortlessly, as if they were not even his, but were already written and just waiting for a willing vessel to speak them.

"Yahweh is my shepherd,
There's nothing I need.
He leads to lush pastures,
Takes me to the stream.

"Strengthens when I'm tired.
Guides me the right way.
For all see his kindness,
They'll honor his name.

"Though in death's dark valley,
No danger I fear.
Your shepherd's staff guards me,

I'm safe, for I'm near.

"In full sight of my foes,
You prepare a feast.
Anoint me as if king,
Though I'm but the least.

"Your goodness and love will,
Pursue me all days.
I stand with you Yahweh,
Both now and always."[22]

The tune came to a close and David lay back on his stone. A part of him felt thoroughly contented—and even more so for the song—while the other, rational, somewhat disconnected part was wondering what had just happened, where the song had come from, and what it all meant.

Had Yahweh just played a song through his hands and his voice?

Was it arrogant even to think such a thing?

David pondered this for some time.

Nabal trotted up, seeking a bit of attention.

David scratched behind her ears as he said, "Well, I guess it doesn't matter too much where that song came from, now, does it? It's not like there's an audience for it! I guess these ears of yours will be the only ones that ever hear it."

Satisfied with the state of the back of her ears, Nabal wandered off again. David once again lay back on the stone. A few minutes passed, and he decided it was time to go find that cave.

He sat up and was about to call his sheep, but then he heard one of his sheep call to him.

"Baaa!" it said. It was Nabal. But it wasn't a friendly greeting or a request; it was a scream for help.

It was followed immediately by a much louder, much deeper sound: the guttural roar of a young male lion.

---

[22] Psalms 23

David caught a glimpse of a tail just before it disappeared behind the dense foliage. The other sheep and goats nervously moved closer together.

The ewe's screams continued.

"Nabal!" cried David. He burst into a run.

His right hand instinctively reached into the shepherd's bag. No stones. That's right, he'd used the last one. He cursed himself for being so stupid.

Then he remembered the staff in his left hand, and he ran harder.

He chased the lion through the trees and underbrush, fueled by the cries of Nabal locked in the powerful jaws of the lion. Its movement was slowed by the weight of its prey. He could catch it. He was sure he could catch it.

It seemed to David that the chase lasted only seconds, and yet it stretched out and felt like hours. Small snippets of the past day incessantly ran through his mind.

He saw his mother and the nervous look on her face when he said he would go.

He heard his own voice saying, "I won't lose a single one in my care! Not one!"

He heard his father: "A proper shepherd's staff, just for you."

And he heard his mocking brother, too: "Is a lion like a dog, David, that you would come at it with a stick?"

A stick.

That's what he had in his hand. He could see it even now, as he ran. It had felt so weighty and impressive before. But now ... now that he saw in front of him a nearly four-hundred-pound beast ... now that the lofty and insubstantive imaginings of a little boy met with cold reality of predator and prey ... now that his beloved sheep Nabal was at the mercy of this lion and he was powerless to stop it ... now, it was clear, all of his power amounted to nothing more than a small, worthless stick.

But then, in his mind's eye, he saw something else. He saw Yahweh.

Yahweh smiled.

It doesn't matter how big the lion is, he thought to himself. *And that means it doesn't matter how small the stick is. God is with me, and God doesn't lose.*

Now in striking distance, David swung his staff down on the hindquarters of the lion as hard as he could. The blow landed with a force not his own. The lion's back legs buckled, and it fell and released Nabal from its jaws.

The ewe stumbled but was quickly to her feet and putting distance between herself and her predator. David called to her, but she continued until she'd widened the gap to thirty feet or so. Then she turned around and eyed the lion.

It rose and turned on David.

It leapt at him. He could see the blood of his beloved sheep staining the fangs of the lion as they drew closer.

He grabbed it by the mane and struck with his staff again. This time he directed the blow at the head. It landed with a force so strong he feared it might break his precious new staff. And this time, when the lion fell, it did not get back up.

The fog of adrenaline slowly lifted as he stood over the dead lion. And that's what it was: dead. A lion, an actual lion, killed at his hand with the aid of nothing more than a stick[23].

No, that wasn't right. It was a lion that Yahweh had killed with a stick.[24]

A *stick.*

Fear considered overtaking him, but it felt a little embarrassed now since it had shown up so late to the party. So instead, David laughed, and laughed, and laughed some more, until he was rolling in the dirt with sore stomach muscles and tears streaming down his face.

Nabal stood at a distance and seemed unsure of what to make of all this.

Finally, David quieted and rose to his feet. He dusted himself off and called to Nabal. She ignored him.

He called her again. She ignored him again.

He walked over to the ewe, speaking calmly as he did so, lest she run. He picked her up and put her over his shoulders. Having achieved neither the height nor the bulk of Onan, or any other of the full-grown

---

[23] 1 Samuel 17:34-35
[24] 1 Samuel 17:37

shepherds, he struggled under the weight of the sheep as he made his way slowly back to the rest of the flock, but he was able to stay on his feet, even when he had to perform a rather difficult squatting maneuver to pick up his staff.

He became aware of someone calling out, and it sounded as if it had been going on for some time.

"David? Where are you, my boy? David?"

"Onan?" yelled David. "Is that you?"

"David! Where'd you go off to? Nabal again?"

"Yes, but I've got her," replied David. Then, with a furtive glance back at the lion corpse, he said, "Stay where you are, I'll come to you."

He made his way back through the foliage, moving slowly due to Nabal. He had just struck a lion with such force that it had died immediately, and now he was struggling to carry a sheep, and for some reason these two facts coexisting brought a smile to his face. *Praise God*, he thought.

Onan was visible now. He wore strange expression and he was breathing heavily, as if he had been running.

David was still recovering from the surreal events of the past few minutes, but now he was starting to wonder what the presence of Onan could mean.

"What is it?" said David as he walked up to Onan, a small amount of panic beginning to well in his stomach. "Is everyone okay? Is dad okay?"

"Everything is fine, your father is fine. I've come to get you and I've got interesting news and you've got to move fast, only ... what happened, my boy?"

David was suddenly aware of how he must look. He looked at the staff in his hands and saw the bloodstains. He set it on the ground so he could lower Nabal with both arms. Her coat was stained red at the nape. He looked down at himself and saw the dirt covering his body. He couldn't see his face, but no doubt it was covered in dirt, possibly accented with blood splatter, and framed by two streaks caused by his laughter-induced crying only a couple of moments before.

"I ... I had to save Nabal. I saved Nabal. Yahweh saved Nabal."

Onan looked perplexed. Without a word he headed into the brush in the direction David had come from.

A couple of minutes passed while David waited to see what Onan's reaction would be. He picked up the staff and fiddled with it as Nabal headed back to the rest of the flock. He thought about what to say, but when Onan returned, he still had no idea.

"David …" Onan's voice was a mix of awe and disbelief. "David … David, that was a lion!"

David said nothing. He looked more sheepish than the sheep.

"He's dead, David. He's *dead*! You've … you've … David! Oh, praise God! What could this mean? And with the arrival of Samuel … what could this mean, my boy?"

"Samuel?"

"Yes, Samuel! He's here, at the town! That's why I'm here. You have to go at once!"

"Huh? Why?"

"He wants to see you, David."

"What do you mean? He wants to see dad's family?"

"No, David. That is not what I mean. He does not want to see your family. He's already seen them. He asked everyone in the town to join him for a sacrifice, so we did. But then he started examining every one of your brothers, one after the other, starting with Eliab and working his way down. Then he said to my master, your father, 'Yahweh has not chosen these. Are these all the sons you have?'"[25]

"Chosen?" asked David. "Chosen for what?"

"I don't know, my boy, I don't know. But they sent me to get you right away. Samuel says no one is to sit down to eat until *you* arrive! So, go! Go now, don't wait! I'll watch the flock. Go!"

David set off at a run towards home.

Onan called after him, "And wash yourself in the stream!"

David ran the whole way to town, stopping only briefly at the stream where he'd gathered the stones to quickly dust off his clothes and wash his face and staff.

When he arrived, he entered the town square.

In the center he saw Samuel. The mass of his uncut, grey hair was

---

[25] 1 Samuel 16:10-11

divided into seven long braids.²⁶ In his hand he held a flask. Standing in front of Samuel and talking to him was Jesse, and behind him David's brothers were lined up, as if they were being presented to Samuel. The feast was prepared and waiting, and nearly every member of the town stood in a rough circle around David's family and Samuel.

They noticed him, and soon all eyes were fixed on him. Eliab wore an accusing scowl, as if David had done something wrong, but David didn't know what it was.

He walked slowly towards Samuel.

Samuel gave him long, critical look as he approached. The only sound to be heard in the square was the muted thud of David's sandals hitting the ground with each step. Finally reaching Samuel, David stood in front of his father, who put both arms on his shoulders.

Samuel stared for a minute longer. Then he smiled.

"Yahweh says this is the one.²⁷ What is your name, boy?"

"I'm David. Son of Jesse."

"And you are a shepherd?" said Samuel, eyeing the staff.

"Yes, sir."

Samuel's voice grew louder. He addressed the crowd. "This is the youngest son of Jesse. Look at his brothers! They are tall, handsome, healthy, and strong. When I saw the firstborn of Jesse, I said to myself, 'Surely this is Yahweh's anointed one!' But God said to me, 'No. I have rejected him.'"²⁸

A torrent of barely-restrained emotions exploded within Eliab, but his stone-faced expression hid this from all save those who knew him best. Smiles could be seen on the faces of those in town who were better acquainted with him.

"Yahweh does not judge like we do," Samuel continued. "He does not look at the outward appearance. He looks at the heart. And he has chosen David, a humble shepherd boy, to be a shepherd to his people Israel!"

Samuel turned to David.

"David, son of Jesse, this feast is prepared for you, with your

---

[26] Judges 16:19, Samuel's hair may have been similar
[27] 1 Samuel 16:12
[28] 1 Samuel 16:6-7

brothers and this whole town as witnesses to celebrate with you. And this flask of oil is for you.[29] Come closer."

Jesse took his arms off of his son's shoulders. David took two steps forward.

Samuel held the flask over David's head. "I anoint you, David, son of Jesse"—David closed his eyes as the oil was poured over his head—"King of Israel! God has rejected Saul because he refused to obey him when he fought against Agag and the Amalekites! God brought victory to Israel that day, but Saul sought the approval of his soldiers and satisfaction of his own greed over obedience to his God and kept the plunder for himself. You, David, will be the king of Israel. Saul's power will decrease, and yours will increase. He is placing as his anointed king someone who will guide and protect the people he loves: a good shepherd!"[30]

Yahweh smiled.

---

[29] Psalms 23:5
[30] 1 Samuel 16:13

The Other Daughter

I remember the day I realized it; the day I realized that I was ugly.

It's not something a little girl thinks. My father, Laban, loved me so much. He said all the things a father is supposed to say. "Leah, my precious little girl!" "Your new dress looks beautiful on you!" "There she is, my gorgeous little girl, my firstborn, my love!" He would come in from the fields and hold me in his arms and tell me how beautiful I was. I can still remember the smell on his clothes. The sheep and goats, the earth, my father—these sundry aromas blended together. I've always thought that if love had a smell, this is what it would be.

And so, I remember that day. It burns just to think of it, because I didn't know. I really didn't know. For *so long*, I didn't know. My father told me I was beautiful and I believed him.

It's too bad it wasn't true.

I was thirteen when it happened. I was heading to the well to draw water, and these two men from the town, Elim and Addar, were talking. I had a bit of a crush on Elim at the time. They didn't see me approaching, but on my way I caught a little of their conversation. They were laughing about something.

The first one I heard was Elim. "Wait ... the *same* King Abimelech?"[31]

"Yes!" said Addar.

"No way!"

"It's true!"

"Tell me he didn't try to marry her, too!"

"No, it didn't get that far this time." Addar laughed. "But he did happen to look out a window one day, and what did he see?"

"Ha ha, oh no."

"Yup! That's right, he sees Rebekah kissing Isaac.[32] Oh man, they say he was *pissed*! He calls Isaac in, and he's all, 'She's your wife, I knew it! You're just like your father! What are you *doing* to me? Someone

---

[31] Genesis 20, 26:1-11
[32] Genesis 26:8

could have married her, and then that god you serve, Yahweh, would make us *all* pay for it!'"[33]

The two men laughed for a minute.

They were talking about my aunt, Rebekah. I don't know her well, because she married our relative Isaac and moved away when I was young.

"Man, that's incredible," said Elim, "especially at Sarah's age![34] That family ... wow! Are there more beautiful women in the whole world?"

At this point my heart nearly skipped a beat. I couldn't believe Elim was talking about my family this way, about *me* this way.

Then he said, "What *happened* with Laban?"

"I don't know," said Addar, "but he has his younger daughter, too. It's too early to tell for sure. Maybe she'll be like her aunt?"

I was still giddy from the compliment and I didn't understand what they were saying at first. Even now, even still, after all these years, I can feel the white-hot coal of humiliation burning in my stomach just imagining what they must have thought of me as I approached the well and smiled at them. It was the second most humiliating thing that has ever happened to me. They were shuffling around uncomfortably once they noticed me, and I said hello but they didn't respond. I quietly drew the water. I remember how badly I had to fight the smile that wanted to creep through, because I actually thought they were embarrassed because I had caught them saying how beautiful I was. Beautiful! What an ugly, hideous, cruel word!

It wasn't until I was halfway back from the well before my excited haze dispersed enough that I could play back the last part of the conversation in my head. Then I realized what they were saying. Crushed, I dropped the bucket and ran into the woods, just far enough where no one could see me. My excitement was so quickly replaced with shame and embarrassment that I actually threw up. And then I cried. I don't know how long I sat there crying, alone. It seemed an eternity.

Elim and Addar were saying that I was ugly. I was the shame of my father, Laban, the one hideous blemish on the otherwise perfect record

---

[33] Genesis 26:9-10
[34] Genesis 20:2, 17:17, also note that Sarah was Leah's great-great aunt

of the women in my family. They were saying that maybe my younger sister, Rachel, would turn out like the rest of the women in my family, and would make up for the disappointment that was me. I wished so badly that I had realized this when they were speaking. Maybe I could have snuck away and avoided embarrassing myself in front of them. I still feel sick to my stomach just thinking about it.

I don't know how long I cried after that, and I don't know how many times I cried in the coming days, weeks, and months.

But overtime we learn to deal with these things. I got used to being the "other daughter". That is what people would call me when they thought I wasn't around.

I was old enough to marry, but there were no offers.

In the years that followed, my sister blossomed. She was becoming a young woman, old enough to marry as well. Everyone praised her to my father, but they never said anything about me.

This is when the resentment began to build. Before this, she was just my little sister. My mother had always said that as children we were inseparable. Sure, she was annoying at times, but she was nothing compared to our obnoxious little brothers.

But now I was beginning to hate her. She was the one that all the men looked at, and she knew it.

She hated me too. Our father said he wasn't going to let her marry first, that it "wasn't right to marry off the younger daughter before the older."[35] I think he just wanted to spare my feelings, and, truthfully, I was his favorite and he never made much attempt at concealing that fact. To Rachel, it was all my fault. She couldn't have a family until I did, and who would want to marry me?

Even more time passed and still there were no suitors. My sister and I spent our time helping in the fields with the sheep.[36] It seemed I was resigned to my fate to be husbandless and childless forever.

Through it all, my father kept saying, "Don't worry, my beautiful daughter"—the word "beautiful" stung every time, but I never dared to tell him that—"I will find you a husband. And not just any man, a man worthy of you, my dear." He was always saying things like this, always

---

[35] Genesis 29:26
[36] Genesis 29:9

making promises he couldn't keep, not just to me but to everyone. He was trying to help, I know, but it wasn't any help. None of the men in town showed any interest in me. But still I would smile and try to keep my spirits up. I couldn't bear to disappoint my father.

Then one day a strong and handsome man strolled into town looking for a wife.[37] And that's when everything got much, much worse.

His name was Jacob. He was my relative, the son of my now-famous aunt Rebekah and her husband, Isaac. He was a slim, smooth-skinned man. He spoke little and had a calm demeanor. Beyond this, there was something about him, something that seemed to draw you to him. It was a strange thing. It wasn't that he was handsome, though he was. It wasn't that he was wealthy; in fact, the man really had nothing more than a walking stick.[38] But he had an air about him, something indefinable, something that hinted that this was a man you wanted on your side. I think I know now what that was, but I'll leave that for later in the story.

Of course, who should he happen to meet first? My sister.[39] They were immediately drawn to each other. Perhaps it was because they were both such attractive people. Perhaps they bonded over both being the younger sibling, and both having an older sibling who was clearly favored by their father (I would find out later that Jacob's parents, Isaac and Rebekah, were exceedingly wealthy, and yet they had given him no money or provisions for his trip). Whatever the reason, Jacob was enthralled with her and never even noticed me.

My father accepted him into our house and, true to his nature, immediately put him to work. After he'd stayed for a month or so, I heard about the arrangement he made with my father. He would work seven years in order to marry my sister Rachel.[40]

I remember I was so furious that I actually stormed up to my father, right after dinner, and screamed at him.

"You said, father! You said! I was to be married first, that's what you

---

[37] Genesis 28:1-5, 29:1-13
[38] Genesis 32:10
[39] Genesis 29:9-12
[40] Genesis 29:14-19

said!" I had to fight to keep my voice level, and I wasn't winning that fight.

"Leah—"

"No! I told you! Didn't I tell you? No one wants me! No one! You didn't have to tell me these things, you didn't have to tell me I was beautiful, you didn't have to tell me I'd marry, you didn't have to! I can be happy without a husband! I can! But I *believed* you!"

He pulled me close to him and held me. I caught the smell of his clothes and I wept all the more. Through the sobs I just kept saying, over and over, "I *believed* you, father, you didn't have to say those things, I *believed* you…"

He held me for a few minutes, and my sorrows dulled, seeming to drain out with my tears, because a person can only hold so much of either.

"Leah," he said, gently, "How could I refuse Jacob? He's agreed to work for me for seven years. How could I turn that down? You've seen the man, there's something about him. I think the god of Abraham, Yahweh, watches over him, and you've heard the stories. His father, Isaac, was born to Abraham when he was a hundred years old,[41] and your great-great-aunt, Sarah, was ninety! That family has won incredible battles,[42] they've amassed wealth;[43] nothing they've set out to do has failed! Even in this month Jacob has been working for me you can see how this god has blessed us for taking him in. We haven't lost an animal since he arrived! Think what this could mean for our family!"

I said nothing. My face was still buried in his chest. I couldn't bear to look at him.

"You will marry first, Leah. We have seven years. I will find you a man just as good as Jacob. And he'll work just as hard for you as Jacob will for Rachel! I promise you!"

Some in the town said my father was a schemer, a swindler, a trickster, but I never believed them when I was little. To me, he could do no wrong. But, for the first time in my life, I was beginning to see

---

[41] Genesis 21:5
[42] Genesis 14:14-16
[43] Genesis 12:5, 12:16, 13:2, 13:5-6, 14:23, 20:14, 20:16, 26:12-14, 26:28-29

that there was some truth to what they said. It seemed that his promises to me had vanished as soon as he thought there might be some profit to be made. But what could I say?

The next seven years passed uneventfully. I was now resigned to my fate. Somehow that made me feel better. My father was still promising to get me a husband, and I would smile and nod in a manner that I hoped seemed appreciative, but I never once believed him.

Meanwhile, our family's wealth grew tremendously.[44] It was hard to say why. It just sort of ... happened. The sheep and goats miscarried less frequently, food seemed to stretch a little farther, the myriad of occasional small losses that would plague our neighbors didn't seem to happen to us. Jacob's flock prospered most of all. His animals bore twice as many young as those that were put under my or Rachel's care. They were healthier and stronger, produced more wool, endured less attacks; everything went better for them.

Our younger brothers were starting to come of age now and becoming shepherds themselves. Father preferred having them learn under Jacob, even over himself.

As my father's wealth increased so did his stature. He had already been a leading man in the city, but now he was becoming the most respected man for miles around.

My father said it was all because of the god of Jacob, this "Yahweh". It didn't make any sense to me. I'd seen my father, as well as many others in the town, serving various gods, but it never seemed to do them any good. Why should this Yahweh be any different? And if he was so great, why were we serving all of these other gods?

The seven-year period finally ended. I was still unmarried. I had made my peace with it though. Some of my resentment for Rachel had even dissipated and in its place I was finding room to be happy for her.

Then the morning of the wedding feast came. I was already filled with a torrent of emotions that I had no idea how to handle when my father sent for me. When I arrived, his expression seemed almost to match how I was feeling.

Standing quietly next to him was Zilpah, one of the servants. She

---

[44] Genesis 30:27

didn't share the apprehension of my father. She only wore a slightly puzzled expression.

"Leah," he said, "do you love me?"

"Yes, father, I love you."

"Will you obey me?"

"Yes, father, you know I will."

"No matter what?"

"No matter what."

The worried lines on his face lightened somewhat. "Good. You've been a good daughter to me, right up to the end. I told you I would find you a husband. Today I fulfill that promise."

He paused, as if waiting for me to say something. But I didn't know what to say. I couldn't believe what I was hearing.

"You will marry Jacob today, not your sister," he said.

He paused again, but again I didn't know what to do with this. Had my father convinced Jacob, somehow? Or was he going to tell Jacob that he had to marry me, not my sister? Did it even occur to him that I might not *want* to marry a man who loved my sister?

He continued. "Only, I need you to do something for me. Remember that you said you would obey me, no matter what. No matter what, Leah. Remember that."

Zilpah's bewilderment seemed to grow. A sick feeling was beginning to well in my stomach.

"You must not say anything to Jacob," he said. "Or anyone else. I will talk to Rachel myself. All you need to do is go to the feast today and say nothing. Afterwards, I will send for you and you will go to Jacob."

"But Jacob knows?" I asked, without much hope. "You told him?"

"Leah, just do as I say. I love you, you can trust me."

"Father ..."

"You said you would obey. Look, here is Zilpah. She's been a fine servant to me, and now she will be a maidservant to you.[45] No more working in those fields! That's no life for the wife of a man like Jacob!"

He smiled at me. To this day I can remember every facet of that

---

[45] Genesis 29:24

smile; the creases around his eyes, the way his lips parted and showed his upper teeth but not his lower, the way he slightly tilted his head. It's a permanent image burned in my mind. He was genuinely happy. How could he be happy about something so terrible?

"Father, I can't! I can't go to Jacob! He'll be expecting Rachel! Who knows what he'll do?"

"It will work, Leah. It will work."

"He worked for seven years for her! Will he suddenly forget what she looks like? Will he say, 'Oh, it's just Leah, but I guess that's all right.' Father, this is *crazy*!"

"*Leah*!" The word came out with the force of a hammer and the sharpness of a knife. I should have known better. I'd seen women severely beaten for less. My father had never done anything like that, but you never knew.

His voice tendered as quickly as it had hardened. He brought me close to him and hugged me.

"Leah, it will be okay. This is your last day as an unmarried shepherdess. After today, you will be a princess. Just listen to me and get through today. It will all work out."

"Yes, father." The words came automatically. What else could I say?

"Good. Good girl." He turned to Zilpah. "Serve her well as you've served me, girl. This is a good house you're going into. This god Yahweh blesses everything Jacob does. That blessing may extend to you, too."

And then he sent me away.

The rest of the day passed like a dream. Events happened all around me; feasting, dancing, celebrating, and many meaningful looks from my father.[46] I can't imagine what Rachel was feeling. Honestly, I wasn't even thinking about her. It all flowed right around me as I was lost in my own miseries.

What stung most of all was this talk of Yahweh. I seriously doubted the other gods even existed, though I was certainly careful not to say that to anyone. Yahweh seemed to be the only god capable of doing anything. For some reason, that made me blame him all the more. Why

---

[46] Genesis 29:22

not me, too? Every man I'd ever met—save for my father—thought nothing of me. Did this god not see my misery? Did he not care? Was he only good for blessing sheep and goats? Was it only men that he cared about?

Then, later that evening, when the sun had set, the festivities were over, and everyone had gone home having had way too much to drink, my father came to me in my room.[47]

"This is it, Leah," he said, in hushed tones. "Here, put this on." He handed me a veil and dress. "I'll be right out here, just come out when you are finished dressing."

When I had come out of my room, he said, "Good. Good! Leah, you look so beautiful, even in this dim light! Come on, let's go see your husband."

The encouraging tone of his voice could not belie the treachery we both knew was taking place. I wanted to scream at him. I wanted to run away. How could he possibly think this would work? How could he possibly think this was a good idea? How could he do this to Jacob and Rachel? How could he do this to *me*?

As we walked he just kept talking in a quiet, calm, and encouraging tone, as if he could hear my thoughts. "Just a little farther, Leah. That's all. You've been a wonderful daughter to me. Now it's time for you to start a family of your own. I love you, Leah. That dress looks beautiful on you. Now, listen to me just a little longer. Don't say anything to Jacob. Don't utter a single word. He's had enough to drink tonight. He won't know. Trust me, Leah. Just a little longer."

We walked out of the house and into the night sky.

"I've had Jacob's tent set up not far from the house. Just trust me, Leah. Just a little farther."

For all the raging anger and humiliation inside me, I said nothing. We reached the tent. My father had me stand back a few feet as he spoke into the dark tent.

"Jacob," he said, "today you become my son-in-law. You have worked seven years for my daughter, and here she is. May Yahweh continue to bless us, and may he bless my daughter with so many

---

[47] Genesis 29:23

descendants that no one can count them, just as he promised your grandfather, Abraham."

For the briefest moment, amidst all the inner turmoil, a flash of hope appeared. Children! I had given up on ever having this joy. Perhaps ... but no. Reality flooded back in and overwhelmed this tiny spark of hope. What good could possibly come of this?

My father sent me into the tent and left.

I will not describe to you the events of that night, save that he did not discover who I was. The nervousness and humiliation were overwhelming.

Then the morning came, and with it came sunlight that revealed all to a man who was now sober.

I said before that when I overheard Elim and Addar speaking at the well, it was the second most humiliating thing that ever happened to me. It did not compare to that moment in the morning when my husband—and that's what he was now—woke up and turned and saw my treachery.

He looked at me first with a puzzled expression, then with realization, then with disgust, and finally with anger. Wordlessly, he got up and stormed out.[48]

My own husband found me repulsive.

Where could I turn now? My father had sent me away from the household I had known ever since I was a little girl. My husband couldn't bear to look at me. I had no possessions to speak of. I was alone and unloved and ...

For a short while I sat there, too numb to even cry.

"Ma'am? Leah?" The voice came from outside of the tent.

"Zilpah?" That's right, the maidservant my father had given me, I had almost forgotten about her.

"Leah, I have important news."

I did what I could to get myself together and came out of the tent. Zilpah was standing there apprehensively.

"What is it?" I asked.

"Jacob just confronted Laban. Jacob is such a quiet man. I have

---

[48] Genesis 29:25

never seen him so angry. But Laban told him that it wasn't our custom to marry the younger daughter before the older. Then he said he could marry Rachel too, after the bridal week is over, in exchange for another seven years of work."[49]

I remembered again what I'd overheard the villagers say about my father: schemer, swindler, trickster.

"This was his plan," I said. "This was his plan all along. No matter how hard he tried, he couldn't find someone who would marry me. So he tricked Jacob and got fourteen years of service in the process. If Jacob is as successful for the next seven years as he was the last, father will be wealthy almost beyond measure. And I will have nothing, not even a husband. Not really, at least. Jacob cares nothing for me. My father sold me for so many sheep.[50] I have no one. I have nothing."

Pleadingly, I looked at Zilpah. The words came slowly and almost monotonously. "There is no one to turn to. I have no hope. What do I do?"

For a while she said nothing. I stared at her and it occurred to me how young she was. I was pleading for advice from a servant, and a mere girl at that.

Just as I was beginning to feel foolish, she spoke. "Perhaps ... you can seek help from a god."

"The gods do nothing." I hesitated slightly, but she was only a servant after all. "I'm not even sure they actually exist. I think it might all be made up stories."

I'd never said that out loud before. I knew it to be true, lots of people knew it to be true, but no one ever *said* it. It was almost a relief to utter the words.

Zilpah reflected my relief. There was no one around, but she almost whispered, "I would not have said anything if you hadn't."

"So then what help could I get from seeking a god?" I said.

"There's Yahweh. He seems different. You know all the stories about Jacob's family. I wouldn't have believed them before but look how wealthy Laban has become. I've heard Jacob talking about him. Surely you have too. He speaks like Yahweh is not only *a* god, he's *the*

---

[49] Genesis 29:26-27
[50] Genesis 31:15

God! Jacob says Yahweh created everything! He says there's nothing Yahweh can't do! And ... I think it's true! I think he's real! If you prayed to him, maybe he would help."

"Oh, he's real, is he? He's real?"

Now my jumbled emotions slowly began to coalesce and compact into one tiny, focused fire of anger. The words came fast now. Inhibitions were completely overcome.

"If he's real, then he sees my father getting wealthy at the expense of others. If he's real, then he sees Jacob being left with nothing while my father gets rich selling his two daughters! My father mentioned him last night. He told Jacob, 'may he bless my daughter with so many descendants that no one can count them, just as he promised your grandfather Abraham.' If he's real, then on the heels of that *blessing* from my father came the most humiliating day of my life! And if he's real, then he sees my pain every day but does nothing! And if he's the creator, then he's not only guilty of ignoring my misery, he actually put me here!"

I realized that, in my rage, I had taken a few steps forward and forced Zilpah backwards. The girl was terrified. I made an effort to soften my expression and relax my stance. "I'm sorry. It's not your fault. Please ... just go."

"Yes, ma'am." The scared girl left quickly.

My bridal week—if it can fairly be called that—passed quickly. It wouldn't be right for Jacob to be out in the field during this time, so he busied himself around the tents and house. He spoke little to me. I approached him twice, but he would not lie with me again.

A week passed and he married Rachel, too.[51] Our father gave her a maidservant as well, a girl named Bilhah.[52]

After that, Jacob had almost nothing to do with me.[53]

Now, as the wife of a man like Jacob, it wouldn't be right for me to help out with the sheep anymore. Instead I prepared meals, helped with the grain, mended clothes, and just generally found anything I could to keep busy. Meanwhile, my sister openly detested me. Now

---

[51] Genesis 29:28
[52] Genesis 29:29
[53] Genesis 29:30

that she was so clearly the favored one from our husband, she treated me as little more than a servant. Jacob barely acknowledged my existence.

My sister and I both had separate tents, but she slept every night in Jacob's.

Zilpah stayed in my tent with me. I cried every night, but there was no one to hear me but her. Zilpah, when she could bear it no longer, would again tell me to try praying to Yahweh. I refused every time.

Shortly afterwards, it became clear that I was pregnant.[54] When I first mentioned to Zilpah that I had missed my period, she nearly squealed with glee.

"Leah!" she said. "Perhaps Yahweh has seen your misery, even though you refuse to pray—oh, sorry ma'am, it's not my place."

"It's okay, Zilpah. I'm really just a servant in this house too, aren't I?"

"No, Leah! You have a child now! And if Yahweh has granted you this favor, even after Jacob refuses to be with you, surely he'll protect this child and keep him safe."

"Him?" I asked.

Zilpah flushed, but only slightly. "Just a hunch. Just imagine it! The first son of Jacob will be yours."

I laughed, ever so slightly. A laugh, coming from me ... it felt strange. But it didn't last long. "Maybe then he'll love me," I said, without much feeling.

"But," said Zilpah in a much smaller voice, "you know ..."

"What is it?"

"It's just that, ma'am, I know it's not my place, ma'am, but it seems to me, ma'am—"

"Oh, Zilpah, just spit it out already! I told you, I'm little more than a servant just like you."

Zilpah rallied. She spoke very quickly, as if afraid she wouldn't have the courage to finish. "Perhaps you should be focused on Yahweh instead of Jacob. Maybe Jacob doesn't love you, but it was Yahweh who allowed you to be pregnant anyway."

---

[54] Genesis 29:31-32

"Why are you so sure this is Yahweh's doing?" I said. "Women and men lie together and have children. It's the way of the world. I was with Jacob and now I'm going to have a child. What does Yahweh have to do with it?"

"Well, you said a few weeks ago that if he was the only God, and if he was the creator, then everything that has happened to you is his fault. Will you blame him for the bad but give yourself credit for the good? Men like Jacob and Laban are mistreating you but God is blessing you in the midst of it. Will you blame God and not them?"

I had to bite back the angry response that threatened to come out. I had told Zilpah she could speak openly with me. She was about the only friend I had at that time.

"Maybe," I said.

Zilpah smiled brightly in response. I couldn't help but smile as well.

"Okay, okay, how about this?" I said. "If this child does indeed live, and if he's—I mean it's, now you've got me doing it—healthy and strong, then ... well then maybe this god ... we'll see."

It sounded lame to me, but Zilpah smiled even wider, nodded, and headed off to her work.

It was some time yet before Jacob knew. I wanted to be sure that I wouldn't lose the child early in the pregnancy. He paid so little attention to me that he didn't notice anything early. It was only when I was clearly showing that I finally brought it up.

It was a strange moment. He was clearly delighted. I don't think he ever spoke so much to me before that. And he made a fuss over me too: Was my bed comfortable enough? Was Zilpah doing a good job? How long should we wait to tell my father? Were there any special foods or clothes that I needed?

For the first time I mattered to my husband. But I knew that it wasn't me, really, but the child that he cared for.

I told my father soon afterwards. He was so excited, he promised to throw a celebration when the child was weaned, complete with feasting and singing and dancing.

My sister, on the other hand, was not so pleased. I didn't tell her myself; she found out from Jacob. She didn't speak to me for days. I wish I could say that I responded with forgiveness and understanding, but that would be an enormous lie. The truth is that I strutted around the place with my belly stuck out like some kind of decadently plumaged bird. I would find every little opportunity to rub it in her face: "Oh, I'm sorry, can you pick that up for me? It's so hard for me to bend over now, you know, because of the *baby*." "Goodness! What a kick that was! This *baby* must be a strong one!" "I'd better sit for a while. Carrying around a *baby* all day is hard work."

The pregnancy passed without incident and the time finally came for the child to be born. Zilpah, along with some more experienced women in town, was there with me through the labor and the birth. Not surprisingly, Rachel was absent.

When I had delivered, Zilpah picked up the child and said, "I told you, look, a son!"

"Then," I said, weakly, "his name is Reuben.[55] Yahweh has seen my misery after all. Perhaps now Jacob will love me."[56]

He didn't, of course. Shortly after I gave birth he started asking for me instead of my sister in the evenings, but I did not delude myself into believing this would last any longer than until I was confirmed pregnant again. Rachel had not been able to have a child[57]—the women in town were beginning to notice and the gossip was already starting—so Jacob believed that his only chance for children was through me. I'm sure it enraged my sister, but she said nothing about it.

I never stayed until morning, because Reuben needed me. But I was there for a little while afterward, anyway. He would talk to me about his day. He would tell me how the flock was doing. He would talk to me about my father and how hard he worked him. He talked about Yahweh all the time as well.

It was a conflicted time for me. In truth, I immensely enjoyed our talks, but at the same time I felt pangs of guilt at enjoying them. Why should I be kind to this husband who didn't love me? Why should I pine after his affection when he cared nothing for mine?

Very soon afterward I was pregnant again. As I suspected, this

---

[55] Reuben means "look, a son" and sounds like the Hebrew for "he has seen my misery."
[56] Genesis 29:32
[57] Genesis 29:31

proved to be the end of my evenings with Jacob. Things went back to the way they were before. I was again little more than a servant, except that now I had a son to look after. He was exhausting, yet I don't think anything has ever brought me so much joy.

Meanwhile I was beginning to look to Yahweh more and more. I had all but abandoned the other gods, though I was careful not to say anything to others in the village. My father's household gods now were nothing more to me than little carved figures. I noticed Jacob had no such things. There was no shrine or monument either; when he had some request of Yahweh he would just go into his tent or up on a hill, or sometimes stay right where he was, bow to his knees and talk to him. It was very strange and yet it made a strange kind of sense. Jacob seemed to just assume that Yahweh was always with him.

I started doing this as well. Even though I still wasn't so sure about Yahweh, the evidence of his blessing on Jacob—and to some degree on me—was hard to ignore. Not having some ritual to go through or shrine to go to or figure to bow before was unsettling at first but I quickly got used to it. I never heard anything audible but I could sort of *feel* him. He brought me comfort, joy, and peace. Some problems I brought to him would solve themselves in unexpected ways, others would remain and yet didn't seem so problematic anymore, still others seemed to go unanswered but he always seemed to give me just enough strength to get through.

The time came and my second child was born without issue, just like Reuben. I named him Simeon,[58] because Yahweh had heard I was unloved and given me a second son.[59]

As before, Jacob was with me only long enough for me to conceive, which happened quickly. Then he set me aside again. Still, he would spend time with Reuben and Simeon whenever he could. I just kept hoping that if I gave him more children, maybe at some point he would feel affection for *me* and not just for them. So, when my third son was born, I named him Levi.[60]

After Levi was born, our ritual began yet again, and I was quickly

---

[58] Simeon means "one who hears".
[59] Genesis 29:33
[60] Levi means "feeling affection for". Genesis 29:34

pregnant for the fourth time.

Jacob wasn't any more attached to me than he ever was, but the attitude of others had definitely changed. Having three healthy sons in such a short time and being pregnant for a fourth time was rare enough that people were noticing. My father praised my children and me repeatedly each time he visited (which was growing more frequent; the wealth he was acquiring from Jacob's success and the fact that my brothers were now old enough to work in the fields unsupervised meant that he barely needed to work these days). Women in the village who seemed to barely know I existed before were now greeting me respectfully and making a fuss over the babies. Many of them would come by and help, which was a great relief because even with Zilpah's aid I was having trouble keeping up with all three of them.

The attention that used to go to Rachel was now going to me. She grew even colder and more bitter than ever. I tried to reconcile with her, but most days she wouldn't even talk to me.

About three months after Levi was born, while everyone was aware that I was pregnant again, Rachel came in from visiting some people in the town in a torrent of humiliation and anger. One of the women must have said something to her, but I don't know what it was. That evening, when Jacob came in from the fields, Rachel stormed up to him. "Give me children or I'll die!" she said.[61]

Hot, tired, and hungry; most days my husband was not his usual quiet self when he came in from the fields, and today was no exception. "Am I God?" He was almost yelling. "He's the one who won't let you have children!"[62]

"Bilhah!" Rachel yelled. Her maid was at her side almost instantly. "Here! Take Bilhah as a wife too, and she can have children. I will build a family through her!"[63]

Jacob's attitude changed almost immediately.

He stuttered and protested for a while. He even shot a few furtive glances in my direction; I think he wanted to ask my opinion but was afraid of what Rachel would say. She spent some time trying to

---

[61] Genesis 30:1
[62] Genesis 30:2
[63] Genesis 30:3

convince him, but let's be honest: most men in that position wouldn't require too much convincing. In the end he agreed.[64]

Now I was sharing my husband with two other women, and Bilhah was pregnant almost immediately.

I was reminded of what Zilpah had told me once: "Perhaps you should be focused on Yahweh instead of Jacob. Maybe Jacob doesn't love you, but it was Yahweh who allowed you to be pregnant anyway." I decided that's exactly what I would do. So, when it came time for my fourth son to be born, I said, "This time I will praise Yahweh," and I named him Judah.[65]

To be honest, at this point I thought I had it all figured out. My husband didn't love me, but I thought I could live with that. I had four sons: four healthy, happy, strong little boys who exhausted me (and Zilpah, for that matter) but brought joy to my heart. And despite our father owning everything that Jacob produced, I was never in want of anything and neither were my sons. Did I have a good husband? No. But I had a good *God*.

But after Judah was born, things changed. With Bilhah now so far along in her pregnancy, Rachel had become completely insufferable. No longer did she make subtle, passive-aggressive remarks at my expense; now she was firing full-blown, unveiled insults at me with any opportunity she could get.

Truthfully, that didn't bother me, at least any more than usual. What bothered me was that Jacob never asked for me like he did after the first three births.[66]

When the time came for Bilhah to deliver, it was now clear to me that Jacob was completely shutting me out. I tried to be happy for Bilhah and my sister anyway. I even came to help out with the labor and delivery, but Rachel screamed at me and sent me out.

Right after the delivery I came to get a look at the child. Rachel held him amidst a gaggle of women smiling and complimenting her. When

---

[64] Genesis 30:4
[65] Judah sounds like the Hebrew word for "praise". Genesis 29:35
[66] Genesis 29:35. It's possible Leah stopped having children despite continuing marital relations, but the events of Genesis 30:14-16 may imply they weren't having relations at all.

she saw me, she smiled an evil smile. She came close to me so that she was out of earshot of everyone else.

"So, it seems God has vindicated me and given me a son," she whispered. "I've named him Dan."[67]

"Congratulations, Rachel," I said. "I'm happy for you." I tried to convince myself that I meant it.

Her voice took on a scathing tone. Her smile stayed glued to her face so that none of the other women would know, but every word was hissed out. "Now Jacob will see that he doesn't need you. I've told him to stay away from you. We can build a family through Bilhah. He can have his wife, his *real* wife, the one he intended to marry all along, the one who didn't trick him into marry her like the little *wretch* that she is. Jacob is mine now. You can just go back to being the little servant you are."

The words crushed me but I wasn't going to give her the satisfaction of knowing that. I smiled, said congratulations one more time, and walked away, making every attempt with casual body language to mask my inner feelings. I realized that I had been waiting for the final nail in the coffin of my marriage—even despite our children—because the experiences of my life had taught me not to trust in hope, even when things looked good. And now it felt like this was it. She had found a way to separate me from him completely.

That day I hatched a plan. Looking back on it now, I think it was wrong, but I didn't know what else to do.

The next day, when Jacob came home, I was waiting for him with Zilpah by my side.

"Here," I said. "If I am unappealing to you, then please take Zilpah as a wife so I can continue building our family through her."[68]

I remember how hurt I was that he didn't say anything to refute the "unappealing" comment. I was desperately hoping he would at least tell me that it wasn't me, that he was avoiding me for the sake of my sister's feelings. It would still have hurt, just not as much. I shouldn't have expected it, but again I had hoped and again I was let down.

Just like with Rachel and Bilhah, he protested for some time but

---

[67] Dan means "he vindicated". Genesis 30:6
[68] Genesis 30:9

didn't *really* put up a fight. Ugh, men.

I never asked for Zilpah's permission. I never even asked her what she thought of the idea. And we never talked about it afterward. But she didn't seem to harbor any resentment towards me. Perhaps she really was just that forgiving, or perhaps with such a self-centered mistress like me she thought her only chance at a family was to be a part of ours.

My scheme worked. Jacob took her as a wife and she was almost immediately pregnant. I had found a way to continue having children through my servant, just like Rachel had through hers.

Bilhah was also pregnant again at the same time.

Bilhah delivered only a few days before Zilpah, and now there were seven little boys in our house. Rachel named Bilhah's child Naphtali,[69] saying, "I've fought with my sister, and I'm winning!"[70] I named Zilpah's son Gad,[71] because I felt so fortunate to be having more children.[72]

This would prove to be Bilhah's last child, but Zilpah was pregnant again almost immediately.

At this point the whole town was talking about us. My father's wealth continued growing ever larger because of Jacob's work, and now Jacob had seven sons after only four years of marriage—it was unheard of! Everyone knew the stories about Abraham beating entire armies and Sarah having a child at ninety, but now they were seeing the work of Yahweh firsthand. Women would come by to ask all sorts of questions about him: Was he some kind of fertility god? What sort of carved image did they need to make? What sort of rituals would they have to go through?

I explained to them everything I knew about Yahweh; that he didn't appear to live in any temple and he didn't ask you to bow down to some little statue made by a human. He was just ... everywhere. He was more powerful than all the others gods. With a select few who I trusted, I even dared to say: he's the only God.

---

[69] Naphtali means "my struggle".
[70] Genesis 30:7-8
[71] Gad means "good fortune".
[72] Genesis 30:10-11

Our family was enjoying the favor of everyone around us and I was no exception to that. But at the same time, I was feeling more and more empty inside. Jacob hadn't touched me since Judah was born. He'd tossed me aside to please my sister. All I had in the world were my kids: Reuben, Simeon, Levi, and Judah, along with Zilpah's son, Gad. I was grateful to God for them, but I still felt so alone.

Zilpah eventually gave birth a to a second son and I named him Asher[73] because of the great joy he brought to us.[74]

I'm getting ahead of myself, however, because three months before Asher was born a very strange event took place.

I was out in a field letting the kids play. Judah, my youngest, was about a year and a half, and he was toddling around and babbling in that delightful way kids his age do. My oldest, Reuben, was four-and-a-half. Zilpah was not with me; she had enough work of her own being pregnant and taking care of a six-month old.

Amidst the children playing I sat down and prayed to Yahweh, as I was in the habit of doing. For over two years my husband had barely acknowledged my existence. I begged Yahweh for *something*; some sign, some encouragement, something that said that he still saw me and cared for me and that my misery would end.

While I was praying, Reuben came up and began tugging at my sleeve. Of course, being four years old he was completely oblivious to what I was doing. He told me he had a present. He handed me some mandrakes that he'd found.[75]

I sat there for some time turning the mandrakes over and over in my hand. I mean, it was certainly quite a find. Mandrakes should have been out of season about a month prior to this, and since a lot of people in the area used them for various remedies and it was so late in the season they should fetch a high price if I wanted to sell them.

But, really? I ask God for a sign and he gives me ... mandrakes?!

I should have known. God is so clever. He takes hopeless situations and turns them into tremendous blessings. It would be just like him to rescue those who love him with nothing more than a vegetable.

---

[73] Asher means "happy".
[74] Genesis 30:12-13
[75] Genesis 30:14

When my sister saw the mandrakes, she asked me for some. Again, I wish I could say that through all of this I'd acted nobly and kindly and with great forgiveness. But ... no. Instead I said, "You steal my husband and now you want to steal my son's mandrakes?"[76] I turned and walked away with a smug air.

Rachel followed after me. "Ugh. Okay, listen. How about this: if you give me some of the mandrakes, you can sleep with Jacob tonight."

I stopped and pondered this for a second, but then I decided I'd better act quickly before she changed her mind. I turned. "It's a deal!" I said, as I shoved some of the mandrakes into her hand.

That evening when Jacob came back, I was waiting for him. I did my best impression of a woman being coy. "Jacob, you must spend the night with me tonight. I've hired you with some mandrakes my son found."[77]

He shot a glance at Rachel. I didn't see her, but she must have nodded affirmation, because he turned back and said, "Ok," in a tone that carefully gave nothing away.

That's when everything changed. I realize now that God was working towards this all along, but at the time I didn't see it. Not only was I pregnant again immediately—praise God—but the next day I overheard Jacob and Rachel speaking. He was very angry with her.

He said to her, "I have been mistreating her for your sake! You told me if I loved you I wouldn't be with her anymore. You claimed this was so important to you, yet you gave it away for a few mandrakes! I have sinned against her, but I won't any longer. She is my wife as well."

They never found out I'd overheard them. Jacob also never bothered to tell *me* that he'd wronged me or ask *my* forgiveness, but nevertheless from that day forward he treated me very differently. No longer was he cold and uncaring towards me. Rachel was still the favorite, but he treated me with kindness, respect, and honor.

I gave birth again, and then nine months later yet again. I named them Issachar[78] and Zebulun,[79] because I believed God was rewarding

---

[76] Genesis 30:15
[77] Genesis 30:16
[78] Issachar means "reward".
[79] Zebulun probably means "honor".

me for giving Zilpah to Jacob as a wife.[80] I realize now that it was probably foolish, but at the time that's what I thought.

I was immediately pregnant one more time. This would turn out to be the last, but of course I didn't know that when it happened.

During these last three pregnancies I was convicted to try to restore my relationship with my sister. We had been bitter rivals for so long that I barely knew where to start. It was rocky at first, but over time—what felt like a long, long time—she began to warm to me.

And then a singular event happened.

Shortly into my last pregnancy Rachel came to me. She was clearly fighting some internal struggle just being there. Her voice quivered. Her eyes watered.

"Leah," she said. "It's been over six years and still I'm childless. The women in the town talk about me when they think I can't hear. They used to say I was beautiful! They used to compare me to Sarah and Rebekah! Now they say I'm cursed. I don't know what to do. I've tried all sorts of medicines and remedies. I've consulted with every one of father's household idols. I've tried Jacob's god too. Nothing works.

"Jacob tells me not to worry, but I know it bothers him too. He says the same thing happened with both Sarah[81] and Rebekah.[82] He says his god will bless me eventually. But look at Zilpah and Bilhah! Look at you! You've already had six sons, and you're pregnant again! My husband has ten children and I have had nothing to do with it! Sarah and Rebekah did not have to deal with this misery."

She sat down on the ground.

"I don't know what to do," she said.

I sat with her but didn't speak at first. It was such a strange thing to see her coming to me like this. For so long I'd been wrapped up in my own miseries that I was blind to the struggles of anyone else. I'd felt cursed even while Yahweh blessed me well beyond any woman I knew. I'd felt beaten and humiliated by my sister even while everyone praised me and shamed her.

"I think it's Yahweh you need to seek," I said, after some time. "He

---

[80] Genesis 30:17-20
[81] Genesis 11:30
[82] Genesis 25:21

can bless you."

"I told you I already tried. It doesn't work. Nothing works."

"You treated him like the other gods. He's not like them."

Now the sarcasm entered her voice, but I tried to ignore it. "Oh, sister, then tell me: what is he like?" she said.

"He's not like them. He's not a god of fertility, or a god of the water, or a god of the hills, or a god of the mountains. He's *the* God, he's the God of everything. He's Yahweh, God."

Rachel buried her head into her knees. She was sobbing quietly.

"It's like ... remember when we were kids," I continued. "Father loved us very much and gave us what we needed. But that doesn't mean he always gave us what we asked. He might say no if he thought it would be bad for us.

"I think Yahweh is like that. He's like a father, only, in heaven.

"When we were little girls, imagine what would have happened if you'd gone to every man in town and said, 'Father, if you love me, will you please give me some jewelry?' And then, after talking to all of them, you finally went back to your *real* father and said, 'Father, if you love me, will you please give me some jewelry?' Would he give you what you asked? No. He would be indignant. He has earned the title 'father', no one else has. He's provided for all of your needs, he's sacrificed for you, he's patiently taught you, he's loved you through hard times and good times. And other men, if you were to view them as your father, would not treat you as well as he would. So, calling other men 'father' is both and insult to him and harmful to you. A good father would correct you, because love demands it.

"So, with Yahweh ... He's the creator of all things. There is nothing he can't do. He is good and cares about us. He's like our father in heaven, and he won't share the title of God with anyone or anything because if he did he would be a bad father to us."

Rachel did not respond. I had no idea how she might be feeling. It seemed like she was balanced on a thin wall, with permanent anger and rejection on one side and submission to God on the other. I was afraid that even the slightest nudge might push her the wrong direction.

I chanced to offer to pray with her. She said nothing yet again, which I chose to take as a reluctant yes. I prayed and asked God to take away her shame and give her a child. When I was finished she did as well.

My prayer was flowery; it was long and rambling and filled with the little meaningless but nice-sounding terms that I'd built up out of habit over the past few years.

Her prayer was short with simple words filled with pain. It was so much better, so much more honest, so much more like a conversation and not a ritual. My sister taught me how to pray that day.

And, praise God, he answered quickly, and my sister finally had the joy (and the suffering, to my secret delight) of a pregnancy.

About six months later I gave birth to my seventh child. God had completed my joy by giving me a daughter to add to my many sons. I named her Dinah.[83]

My sister gave birth to her first child. Our rivalry was finally truly dissolving, so I was there to help with the birth. What a joyous occasion it was! Despite the exhaustion and pain, I've never seen Rachel happier than when she held that little boy. "God has taken away my disgrace," she said. "Maybe he'll even add another." She named him Joseph.[84]

Around this time the fourteen years were finally up, and Jacob was eager to take us all back to his home.

My father was now so wealthy and had so many servants that he concerned himself with nothing except what to eat and drink. He knew that the reason for that was Yahweh's blessing on Jacob. So, he negotiated with Jacob to stay longer, with the promise that now he could accumulate belongings for his family as well, not just for my father's.

Of course, it was a trick by my father to try to get more out of Jacob and our family without fulfilling his end of the bargain.[85] That's just so like him.

Of course, Yahweh worked things out so that my father's schemes were thwarted and Jacob became wealthy while my father lost more

---

[83] Genesis 30:21
[84] Joseph means "may he add". Genesis 30:22-24
[85] Genesis 30:34-36

every year.[86] That's just so like him.

Within six years,[87] most of my father's wealth had become ours. His attitude towards Jacob had changed, and my brothers really hated him now as well.[88] We eventually escaped from them and headed back to Jacob's home.[89]

Jacob said that if God hadn't protected us, my father would have left with us nothing,[90] and I think he was right. But as it was he had four wives, eleven sons, a daughter, numerous servants and loyal workers, and so many animals they could barely be counted. He came to town twenty years before with nothing more than a walking stick, but when we left there were two large camps.[91]

I remember the last time I saw my father. He said goodbye to all the kids. I kissed him goodbye, too.[92] For all he had done to us—to me—I still loved him. I don't know what has become of him, but I still pray for him from time to time, asking God to forgive him.

Our family has faced many trials since that time, and I am ashamed to say we haven't remained innocent through all of them. My husband now walks with a limp, an injury given to him by God.[93] My daughter, Dinah, was attacked by a man from Shechem, and in response Simeon and Levi slaughtered every man in the town.[94] My sister still clung to false gods, so much so that she stole my father's household gods when we left.[95]

Now, years later, Rachel has died. She gave birth to one more son, but it was her last act. Jacob named him Benjamin.[96]

And now little baby Benjamin, Jacob's twelfth son, perhaps his final son, sleeps peacefully in my arms. His full brother, Joseph, is asleep nearby as well. He's a fine young man. He's technically an adult, but

---

[86] Genesis 30:43
[87] Genesis 31:41
[88] Genesis 31:1-2
[89] Genesis 31
[90] Genesis 31:42
[91] Genesis 32:10
[92] Genesis 31:55
[93] Genesis 32:22-32
[94] Genesis 34
[95] Genesis 31:30-35
[96] Benjamin means "son of my right arm". Genesis 35:16-20

only just barely, and he'll need a mother too. I will be there for both of them.

I don't know what else God has in store for us but I trust him because I know that he loves me. It's not a love like my father's, which is corrupted by greed and pride. It's not a love like my husband's, which I've had to struggle to gain even a little of. It's the love of a true father—my heavenly father.

~

Leah didn't know it at the time, but she was to become the mother of half of the nation of Israel. It was the most influential nation in all of history, God's chosen people, the ones through whom he would bring his message to all peoples of the world.

She was the mother of kings like David and Solomon. And she was the mother of *the* king, the savior of the world: Jesus, the descendant of Judah, the son of Leah.[97]

---

[97] Luke 3:23-33, Matthew 1:1-16

Bold

"Miriam, stir the pot!" the girl mumbled sarcastically. "Miriam, watch Aaron! Miriam, clean the bowls!"

Miriam[98] continued her angry mumbling as she stirred the boiling goat stew just outside a tiny structure that could, if viewed with a tremendous amount of generosity and imagination, be called a "house".

Her mother, Jochebed,[99] stood over her. As with all very thin yet absurdly pregnant women, she gave the impression that at any minute she ought to fall over, yet this was prevented from happening by some complicated physics interaction known only to her feet and back.

"Yes, and after that, *Miriam*, you can go get the bowls. You know how starved your father is when he comes home."

"Ah, *mom!*" Miriam stamped her feet but marched obediently towards the house.

A cry came from inside, emitted by Aaron.[100] It was one of the hundreds of types known to mothers of toddlers. This particular one meant, "I just woke up from my nap and for some reason think the most appropriate response is to start crying unless someone cuddles with me for at least fifteen minutes."

"Oh, and grab Aaron while you're in there," said Miriam's mother.

"Ugh!"

"And stop complaining! Your new sister will be here any day and I'm going to need your help more than ever."

The girl walked into the house and picked up Aaron. He showed his appreciation in the standard toddler fashion by saying, "Mama?"

"Yeah, yeah," said Miriam. "She'll hold you in a second. Let's get the bowls first."

She took the few steps necessary to get from the sleeping-quarter side of the one-room abode to the side with shelves stocked with a humble array of wooden bowls and utensils.

---

[98] Exodus 15:20. It's likely that Miriam is also the sister in Exodus 2:1-10.
[99] Exodus 6:20 and Exodus 6:26
[100] Exodus 6:20, also see Exodus 7:7 for age difference

With Aaron on one hip, she tried to gather up the bowls with her free hand, but dropped them. As she bent over to pick them up, she heard her mother's voice again.

"Miriam, go and get auntie Deleah!"

"*Mo-om*," she cried, "I haven't even finished with the bowls yet! Can't I finish one thing—"

"Stop your backtalk girl and get auntie Deleah!"

"Ugh! Okay! Just one second." Miriam continued trying to gather up the bowls.

"*Miriam!*"

The tone finally caught the girl's attention. She abandoned the bowls and went back outside, still carrying Aaron.

Her mother was sitting on the ground with a pained expression on her face.

"Mom?" Miriam said.

"Mama!" said Aaron.

"It's okay, sweetie," said her mother with forced politeness through clenched teeth. "It's just time for your baby sister to come. I need you to get auntie Deleah as fast as you can, okay? She'll get Puah.[101] If you can't find auntie Deleah, just go and get Puah, okay?"

"Who's Puah?" asked Miriam.

"Never mind. Just go and get auntie Deleah. Take Aaron with you, I don't want him to burn himself and I don't think I can watch him."

Miriam set off at the closest thing approximating a run that a small girl carrying a toddler can muster. Aaron cried (this one meant, "I thought mommy was going to hold me but she's not holding me and it's *so terrible!*").

~

Shortly, a bustle of activity was happening around Miriam's tiny house. She stood outside keeping track of Aaron while her mother labored inside. The occasional cry of a painful contraction carried to her ears.

---

[101] Exodus 1:15

Within an hour her father, Amram,[102] came home. His hands were rough and dust-covered from many hours spent laying brick.

"Dad!" said Miriam as she ran to give him a hug.

"Hey, sweetie," he said with a smile as he returned her hug. "So, it's time for your sister, eh?"

"Yes. Dad?"

"What?"

"How do you know it's a girl?"

A moment passed while they continued hugging but he made no response.

"Dad?" asked Miriam again.

"We ... we don't know, sweetie. We just hope," said her father.

"You want a girl more than a boy?"

"Well, no. Yes. Kind of."

Another silent moment passed.

"Is that because the Egyptians are killing all the baby boys now?"[103] asked Miriam.

Amram released the hug, held her by the shoulders, pushed her gently until she was an arm's length away, and looked into her eyes.

"You knew? Who told you about that?" he asked.

"Everybody knows, dad," was her somber reply.

"Your mother didn't want us to tell you. She didn't want to scare you. I guess you would have found out eventually. Thank God Aaron was born before this mess started."

"Dad, I made you some goat stew."

Miriam impulsively ran inside to grab a bowl, prompting a few admonishments from the women crammed in the tiny house, but she was able to grab the bowl before being shooed out.

Her father picked up the bowl and laughed. "You're a bold girl," he said with a smile.

Suddenly, he grew very serious. He crouched down on one knee so that his face was only inches from hers.

"You're bold and brave! Don't let them take that from you, whatever you do. These cruel Egyptians will try to break you. *Don't let*

---

[102] Exodus 6:20
[103] Exodus 1:22

them! Someday Yahweh is going to rescue us from all this. We will no longer be slaves, but free! And we are going to need bold people like you to lead the way."

The two looked into each other's eyes for a few seconds, but then Miriam noticed her brother.

"Aaron! Don't put that in your mouth!"

~

A few hours later Miriam heard a newborn cry from inside the house. She and her father rushed in.

The women were solemn. Jochebed, Miriam's mother, was crying. There was no joy to be found.

Amram's face fell.

"It's a boy," he said with a voice devoid of emotion. Without a word, he walked out.

Miriam moved closer until she could see the baby. She smiled at the sight of him.

"Mom! He's *so* cute! Look how small his nose is! Mom, it's *so small!*"

"He's beautiful," said Jochebed with tears in her eyes.

"What's his name, mom?"

"I …" was all Miriam's mother said in reply. An uncomfortable silence in the room followed. Every woman present understood. Do you name a child that the Egyptian masters are just going to kill?

"Listen!" said the midwife, Puah, in a stern voice that broke the silence. "Listen to me! This is a fine boy you've got. You have to hide him! Don't let the Egyptians see him! Not all of them would be willing to throw a baby into the Nile but some *will follow* Pharaoh's command! You can't trust anyone! You can't even trust other Hebrews!"

The midwife turned to the other women. "That goes for all of you. Do not celebrate. Do not act any differently. Pretend that this was a tragic stillborn baby!"

They all nodded agreement. Puah turned back to Jochebed.

"And tell your husband to keep working for the Egyptians like normal and not to say a word," she said.

~

Three months passed.[104] The baby grew stronger and healthier. His eyes grew more focused and he seemed aware of things going on around him. He smiled freely and often.

As he grew healthier, Miriam's father grew more distant and her mother more depressed. Miriam understood, even if they didn't think she did. He couldn't be hidden forever. It was only a matter of time before an Egyptian happened to see him and started asking questions, or another Hebrew fed information to one of the task masters in exchange for a modest reward. They would find him and when they did they would throw him in the Nile river, just as Pharaoh commanded.

Even so, Miriam did everything she could to help out her mother with the baby and Aaron.

One day her mother told her to watch Aaron and the baby for a while and went out. She came home shortly with a papyrus basket and a container of ... something. It was black and sticky.

"Are they both asleep?" asked Jochebed.

"Yup!" said Miriam.

"Well, lucky you," said Jochebed.

"Mom, what's that?" asked Miriam, pointing to the something.

"It's for the basket, to make it waterproof."

"Huh?"

Jochebed gave no reply. She sat down with the basket and began applying the substance to the outside of it with a stick.[105] Miriam watched in fascination as the outside of the basket slowly took on a black and smooth finish.

"Mom?" asked Miriam.

"Yes, dear."

"Do you have a name for the baby yet?"

"No. Must you ask me that every day?"

"Can I name him?"

---

[104] Exodus 2:1-2
[105] Exodus 2:3

"No!" said Jochebed, harshly. Then her voice softened, "No, sweetie. Must you ask me *that* every day?"

"I want to call him Wiggles. He wiggles a lot, mom."

Again, her mother didn't respond. Miriam saw her tearing up as she continued preparing the basket.

When it was finished, she set the basket upside down to dry.

"Don't touch this basket, Miriam," she said.

"Okay. But, mom, what are you *doing*?" asked Miriam again.

Jochebed sighed.

"I shouldn't tell you this," she said. "You shouldn't have to live like this. You should be protected from all this. You should be playing and happy and have plenty of food and … *curse those Egyptians!*" Her voice was quiet but filled with rage.

She turned towards her daughter, finally looking into her eyes for the first time since she'd arrived with the basket.

"But, you do have to live like this," she continued. The tears now flowed freely. "I might as well tell you. You know that if the Egyptians find this baby, they are going to kill him. I can't hide him any longer. I don't know what to do. Tomorrow, I'm putting him in this basket and placing it in the Nile. Maybe … somehow … I don't know. I don't know what else to do."

Jochebed sat down and wept.

Miriam approached and hugged her mother, clinging tightly to her for a minute or two.

"Dad says Yahweh is going to rescue us from the Egyptians," said Miriam. "He said we won't be slaves anymore."

Jochebed laughed bitterly. "Wouldn't that be nice," she said, without even the slightest suggestion of hope.

"He can do it though, right mom? You told me he could. You told me he made everything. You told me he blessed Rachel and Leah and they had all those kids—like tons of kids, like so many kids—and they all had plenty of food and stuff.[106] He told Abraham that we would be slaves but then he would set us free."[107]

Her mother only cried in response. Miriam sat with her a little

---

[106] Genesis 29-35
[107] Genesis 15:13-14

while longer.

"Maybe he can rescue the baby too?" said Miriam.

"Maybe," said Jochebed, but Miriam knew she was using her lying-to-make-kids-feel-better voice.

~

The next day Jochebed did just as she said. She placed the baby in the waterproofed basket and brought it out to the Nile. Miriam followed her with Aaron in tow.

Jochebed placed the basket among some reeds so that it wouldn't float away. Then she placed the top on the basket, picked up Aaron, and walked away with tears running down her face.

Miriam watched her go. She found a hiding spot nearby and waited.

A few minutes passed. The baby was crying out now.

"I hope a crocodile doesn't eat him," said Miriam to herself.

A small entourage of Egyptians approached. Miriam couldn't believe her eyes: it was a princess! The Egyptian princess![108]

"Wow!" she said quietly. "She's so pretty! And she's got servants and everything. Gosh, I hope a crocodile doesn't eat her, either."

The princess strode lazily into the water until she was ankle deep. Then she heard the cry of the baby. She looked around until she spotted the basket.

Miriam couldn't hear what she said, but she indicated to one of the servants who ran to grab the basket.

"Is she going to throw him in the Nile?" whispered Miriam to herself. Her heart was pounding.

The basket was brought to the princess. Miriam risked walking closer to overhear what was said. No one seemed to be paying attention to her anyway; all eyes were fixed on the baby in the basket.

"It's ... it's one of those Hebrew babies. *Ohhh*! Look at his cute little nose!"

"Miss," said one of the servants, "your father said—"

"I *know* what my father said!" screeched the princess. "I am not my

---

[108] Exodus 2:5-10

father! And I am *not* killing a baby!"

The princess smiled and looked into the baby's eyes. "Besides ... this may be a gift from the gods. My own child, finally, after all this time!"

The servants looked nervously between them.

One finally spoke up. "He'll need to be nursed, miss."

"Yes," said the princess thoughtfully. "We'll need a Hebrew. None of my Egyptian nurses would do it."

An idea struck Miriam. She stepped forward.

The group saw her and suddenly they were all focused on her.

"I know a Hebrew woman who can nurse that baby for you," she said.

The princess smiled at her. "You do? Wonderful!"

"Shall I go and get her?"

"Yes! And run, girl! Tell her I'll pay her handsomely for her trouble!"

Miriam nodded and then ran back toward her house. Her excitement gave her speed. Her mom would be so excited! God had rescued her brother!

She burst through the doorway, oblivious to all else.

"Mom! Mom!" she yelled.

Aaron—who was just beginning to fall asleep in Jochebed's arms—immediately woke up. Jochebed had tears streaming down her face. In her emotional exhaustion she turned on Miriam.

"What do you want, girl?!" she screamed. She put Aaron down and stepped towards Miriam. "What do you want now? What is *so important* that you must come in and wake up your brother? What is so important that you can't give me just a *few minutes* of peace when I'm so broken and tired and ... what? Come on, what is it! What, you found a spider or something? You want to complain about your chores? You want some extra treat?"

As she raged her voice grew higher pitched and she moved closer to Miriam until she was looming over her.

"*What do you want?!*"

The words came out of Miriam so fast they were barely comprehensible. "The-princess-wants-to-pay-you-lots-of-money-to-watch-the-baby," she said.

Her mother took a step back.

"What?" she said.

"The Egyptian princess! I saw her! She's got all these servants and everything! And she saw the baby and she was like, oh he's so cute look at that baby and his nose is cute too—I told you his nose was cute, mom—and then I said I could get someone to nurse him and she said okay and she's going to give you lots of money to take care of him!"

"What?" repeated her mother.

"Ugh," said Miriam. She walked over to Aaron and picked him up, and then she grabbed her mother's hand and began pulling her back towards the Nile.

"Just come on," she said. "I'll show you!"

Miriam pulled her a few steps before Jochebed finally began walking along unresistingly.

"You're saying the princess wants the baby?"

"Yes!" said Miriam. "And she said she needs someone to nurse it. Only I don't think she knows it's our baby so you probably shouldn't tell her that, but she's really nice and she said she wasn't going to throw him into the Nile or anything."

Her mother said nothing for the remainder of the short trip. As they approached, they saw the princess and her servants fawning over the baby.

Before they had even come close the princess noticed them and walked rapidly to them. The baby was wailing miserably.

Once within earshot, the princess spoke, talking loudly over the voice of the crying baby. "Ah! You must be the nurse this helpful girl told me about! That was fast. Nice job, girl!"

Miriam smiled and did the best impression of a bow that a girl holding a toddler can manage.

"Is this your little one?" said the princess, indicating Aaron.

Jochebed nodded.

"So, you have experience? That's good. Are you good with babies? This poor little guy is so sad! Who knows how long he's been out here in this heat."

Jochebed stammered. "I, uh, I ..." She looked down at Miriam, who gave her an encouraging nod. "I am. I am good with babies, yes."

"Great! And you *are* nursing right? You can feed him?" The princess handed the baby to Jochebed without waiting for a reply. "Here, see if you can get him to calm down. He may be hungry!"

The baby quieted as soon as he was in her arms, soothed by the sight and smell of his mother. The abrupt silence was almost louder than the crying had been.

The princess looked amazed. The servants around her nodded their approval.

"Wow!" she said. "You are *good*! Okay, let's talk details. This boy is to be a *prince*, mind you, so you must take excellent care of him. If he is healthy and survives, then once he is weaned you are to bring him to me. I'll be sending along my servants every day to check on him and to see if you need anything. Oh, speaking of that—"

She put a hand out to one of her servants who stepped forward and filled it with coins.

"Take this," she said, extending her hand to Jochebed. Jochebed's unresisting hand was immediately filled with more money than she had ever seen.

"Hopefully that's enough, at least for now. I'll be sure to send along more when my servants check on you."

She smiled at Jochebed.

"Oh, I've got a good feeling about you! I can't believe how quickly he calmed down after he just met you!"

She smiled and kissed the baby's head.

"Well, you can run along home and I'll send one of my servants so that we know where to find you." She waved a dismissive hand at Jochebed. Then she turned around and headed back to the river. "Now to get back to my bath. Oh, I'm *so excited*! Finally, my own child!"

One of the servants began escorting Jochebed and Miriam away. Jochebed was too shocked to do anything but comply, but Miriam stopped.

"Um, princess?" she asked.

The princess turned around.

"Yes, girl?"

"What are you naming the baby?"

"Naming?" She seemed to give this some consideration. "Well, I drew him out of the water, so ..."

She smiled.

"His name is Moses!"[109]

---

[109] "Moses" sounds like the Hebrew word for "draw out"

Golgotha

It's a strange thing. I feel my body fighting, but my mind is somewhere else.

I see them lashing my arms to the crossbar with rope. I see my arm struggling, every muscle writhing and straining impotently. I hear my voice screaming.

I see the nail. The roman soldier has it now in one hand with his hammer in the other. He places it against my wrist with the expertise of a thousand repetitions. He seems no more concerned than if he were nailing two pieces of wood together.

I hear my voice reach a fever pitch. I see the hammer come down. There's so much blood. How could men survive this for days? There's so much blood.

The rope is removed. The other arm is lashed. The hammer begins its grisly work again.

The centurion in charge talks casually to the soldier with the hammer. "Nice ... right in the groove, no broken bones ... nice and clean. Another fine job, man! That's not coming out!" They laugh.

Now that I'm nailed to the crossbar, they start raising me up to the stipe, the upright part of the cross, affixed in its place at the top of the hill. One of them holds my legs and lets me push up on him. I guess they don't want me to suffocate before I even get up there.

I can hear myself crying now.
The crossbar is nailed to the stipe.
Now they are starting on my legs.
But my mind is somewhere else.

~

I remember when they came. It was only yesterday.

I remember the door bursting open. Barabbas[110] and Jaap were on

---

[110] Matthew 27:16, Mark 15:7, Luke 23:19, John 18:40

the first one through the door and managed to get in a few hits before they were overwhelmed.

I didn't resist. I never do; story of my life. I just go along with whatever is happening. That's probably what led me to this cross.

I didn't resist, but the roman soldiers beat me up a bit anyway. No surprise there.

~

They've finished with my legs. They hurt so much, but I have to push up to get a decent breath. Each time I get a fresh shot of sharp pain in my feet and hands. My back, already stripped raw from the flogging, scrapes against the wood of the stipe. But the alternative is to suffocate.

Now, upright on the cross, I can see the crowd. They stare, some crying, some only shaking their heads, like they always do at these crucifixions. Only they aren't paying any attention to me. No, that prophet guy Jesus is the star of this show.

He's not on the cross yet. They are still working on Jaap. These Romans understand there is a bit of theatrics involved in crucifixions, so they make sure Jesus is front and center, and of course he goes up last.[111] No doubt they would have done the same for Barabbas. I wonder why he's not here.

So that's it then. I'm going to die slowly and painfully, and it matters so little that not a single person is even paying attention to me.

~

I remember the flogging.

They took me from my cell. They stripped me naked. They tied my arms to the wooden poll.

Barabbas was the only one who'd been flogged before. He always downplayed it, said it was no big deal, that he could handle it. He even

---

[111] Matthew 27:38, Mark 15:27, Luke 23:32-33, John 19:18

used to show off the scars.

I tried to convince myself that it was true, but any delusion to that effect was erased with the first lash. You can say this about the Romans: they are artisans in the realm of pain and torture. The whip stripped skin and flesh away. The lead tip on the end added more heft and pain to each strike.

He started on my right side, and worked his way down. Then he moved to the left side. Then he did it again. Then again.

I thought I was going to die. A tiny part of my brain, barely noticeable among the overwhelming pain, was telling me that they wouldn't kill me before the cross. But I couldn't be sure.

Finally, mercifully, it was over.

As they dragged me out, they brought in another man. At first, I thought it would be Barabbas. But, no, it was someone else, someone else where Barabbas should have been.

Oddly, the man was in a purple robe, with a crown made of sticks and thorns jammed onto his head.[112] The soldiers stripped the purple robe from him as he walked.

"Jesus!"[113] said the torturer with a note in his voice that can only be described as gleeful. "The king of the Jews! Your majesty, what an honor it will be to serve you today. Don't worry, you'll get special treatment. It's not often we serve royalty!" I turned my head to see him as he bowed low in mock reverence.

I turned back to Jesus, who was still walking towards me as I was being taken out. They'd already done a number on him. He looked like he could barely stand. Blood was dripping from the top of his head where the mock crown stabbed into his skull. Fresh bruises were all over his face and body.

Jesus didn't seem to pay any attention to the torturer. As he walked by, he just stared at me. I thought perhaps he was looking at me because I represented what was about to happen to him; that he was afraid. Maybe he was. But there was something else, a kind of determined compassion I don't know how to explain, as if amidst his suffering he still was more concerned about me.

---

[112] Matthew 27:28-29, Mark 15:17, Luke 23:11, John 19:2, John 19:5
[113] Matthew 27:26, Mark 15:15, John 19:1

Before they'd even gotten me back to my cell, I heard the screams of pain.

~

Now they are raising Jesus up to the stipe.

The crossbar is secured to the stipe. They begin nailing in his feet. The cries of pain wash over the otherwise silent crowd. Even those crying women who've been following him around all morning are trying to mute their sobs.[114]

The last nail is driven in and the last cry of pain is heard.

"Father!" he cries. "Forgive them! They don't know what they are doing!"[115]

I remember again that look he gave me as he passed me on his way to be flogged. Determined compassion.

The Romans affix the official charge against him above his head. It reads: The King of the Jews.[116]

The sign appears to break the silent spell over the crowd.

"The king of the Jews! Is that really the charge?" says one soldier.

"Yeah," says the man with the sign, "that's what Pilate said."[117]

"That's not right," says one of the Jewish leaders nearby, "it should say that he *said* he was the king of the Jews!"

"Look, pal, this is what Pilate said to write. Take it up with him."

"I think I will!" The indignant Jew stomps off.[118]

Bafflement manages to make its way through my haze of pain. These guys are arguing about two ways of wording the charge, but nobody seems bothered that neither of them is actually a *crime*. Man, this guy must have really pissed off some important people; they can't even think of something to charge him with and they're still killing him.

"Huh," says another soldier. "King of the Jews. Well, your *Highness*,

---
[114] Matthew 27:55, Mark 15:40-41, Luke 23:27, Luke 23:49
[115] Luke 23:34
[116] Matthew 27:37, Mark 15:26, Luke 23:38, John 19:19
[117] Matthew 27:2, Mark 15:1, Luke 3:1, Luke 22:66, John 18:28-29
[118] John 19:20-21

if you are the king of the Jews, why not save yourself? Just come on down from there!"[119]

Another Jewish leader nearby jumps in—one of those arrogant Pharisees. "So, he can only save others? He can't save himself? Oh, come on, if you're a king—*the* King of Israel—just come on down!" He turns to some others in the crowd. "He trusts in God! He even said he is God's *son*! Let God save him if he wants him! If he comes down right now, we'll all believe in him, won't we?"[120]

There is a chorus of hearty mock agreement.

"I heard," says another man, "he said he could destroy the temple and rebuild it in three days."[121]

"I heard him say that too!" says another. "The temple? God's son? Ha! There he is, dying on a cross, just another man subject to Caesar like the rest of us! Some king you are! Messiah!"[122] He spits on the ground.

I can't believe what I'm hearing. No wonder this guy is up there, running around spewing crazy stuff like that.

There is another fresh shot of pain in my feet and wrists as I have to push up to get a deeper breath. The intensity of the pain is beginning to dull ever so slightly, but my muscles are really starting to get sore. I feel like I can't do this much longer. But I know that's not true. I've seen it too many times. Men take *days* to die on a cross.

The crowd continues to mock Jesus and completely ignore me. Some of the stuff they are saying about him, I mean, I just had no idea some of the crazy stuff this guy had said.

Still ... wasn't it only a week ago that they were all praising him?[123]

~

I was there, a week ago, when he entered Jerusalem. It seemed like the

---

[119] Luke 23:36-37
[120] Matthew 27:41-43, Mark 15:31-32, Luke 23:35
[121] Matthew 27:39-40, Mark 15:29-30, Luke 23:35
[122] Matthew 27:17, Matthew 27:22, Mark 15:32, Luke 23:2, Luke 23:35, Luke 23:39
[123] John 12:1, John 12:12

whole world was there.

We were out and about, "working" as Barabbas would have put it. As Passover approached, throngs of people came to the city for the celebration, and with them they brought their money and belongings. It was an ideal time for people like us. The city residents were more cautious, but with those country bumpkins I could snatch their money purse and be a couple of blocks away before they even knew what happened.

We had to be careful though. At that point Barabbas was notorious in the city. Everyone knew about that little incident during the uprising—if it can even fairly be called an uprising. If we got caught ...

I should have known then to get away from him. Barabbas was the one they were after. No one would have come looking for me if I'd just walked away.

I had just finished lifting bit a bit of food from a shopkeeper who was busy exploiting some guy just in from the country. The change in the crowd caught everyone's attention. There was some kind of yelling and cheering happening.

I asked some folks nearby what was going on, but nobody seemed to know. I moved closer to the commotion, pushing through the throngs of people who were all beginning to move in the same direction.

I finally broke the crowd and saw it: a man on a donkey. They were all cheering for a man on a donkey. They were putting down coats and branches on the road ahead of him. He was on a *donkey*.[124]

"What's going on?" I asked someone nearby.

"That's Jesus! The prophet from Galilee!" The man was absurdly excited.

"What? From that thing with Lazarus?"[125] Lazarus lived nearby in Bethany, just outside Jerusalem. *Everybody* had heard about him. The man was dead for days and apparently this guy Jesus brought him back to life.

"Yes! That was him! And they say he did all kinds of other stuff too, like healing blind people and lame people and stuff." The man turned

---

[124] Matthew 21:1-11, Mark 11:1-10, Luke 19:28-40, John 12:12-19
[125] John 11:1-44

to me in a conspiratorial fashion. "They say he put the Pharisees and such in their place a few times too."

"Huh," was all I replied. I had to admit, I liked that last bit. Those muckity-muck Pharisees would never have much to do with me. They were tricky marks too. I guess it takes a thief to know a thief.

The man was almost jumping out of his skin in excitement, like some little kid bobbing up and down.

"What's with the donkey?" I asked.

The guy turned to me. "What?"

"The donkey. What's with the donkey?"

"Man, don't you go to temple?"

"I do, I do," I said. It was only kind of a lie. I've been to the temple plenty of times, especially around Passover. It's an easy place to "work". The moneychangers and the guys selling doves mean a lot of money is moving around.

"Well, the prophet Zechariah spoke about this. He said the Messiah would be riding in on a donkey."[126]

"You think this guy's the *Messiah*?" I said. "The king who's going to kick all the Romans out and take over the world and all that?"

"Well ..." he looked almost embarrassed. Jesus sure didn't look like a king, wearing his simple clothes and riding on a simple donkey. The man rallied. "Who else could have done what he's done? The blind see, the lame walk, he even has power over death! He must come from God, otherwise how could he do all that stuff? And he teaches stuff no one has ever heard before."

Somewhere in the crowd, someone yelled, "The savior! The savior has come from David!"

Another voice cried out, "Blessed be the one who comes in the name of Yahweh!"

And yet another voice, "The savior comes from heaven!"

And then suddenly they were all shouting and praising Jesus in a deafening, joyous roar. The man next to me was yelling at the top of his lungs, praising God and praising Jesus.

It started to wash over me. I wondered if there was something to

---

[126] Zechariah 9:9

this. I could feel myself just on the verge of ...

I noticed his money purse. It hung lazily by his side while his arms were up and he was shouting at the top of his lungs.

Seconds later I was walking away, money purse in hand, guilt the only thing holding back the infectious joy of the crowd that threatened to pull me in.

~

The discomfort and pain are really growing now. I can't move or shift; I can't get comfortable. My back is screaming its pain at me. It feels like things are beginning to swell up back there. It feels like my right shoulder is starting to give out. I keep having to decide between putting weight on my shoulders or on my legs, but both are growing tired.

Again I think, *I can't do this much longer.* But again, I know I can ... I've seen too many men do it.

I wonder what will happen if my shoulder gives out.

The crowd is still mocking Jesus. People come and go. The newcomers each insult Jesus in basically the same way I've already heard many times this morning. There are a few women who've stuck around, sobbing quietly for him. There are a few men too—they stand far off, but I see them. They haven't left all morning.

I wish so badly I had someone to talk to. I've got to get my mind off of this.

Just think of something, I say to myself. *Anything.*

~

Barrabbas stood just at the edge of the corner, watching the lone Roman soldier.

He whispered to Jaap and me, "Just a few more seconds."

~

No! No. Not that. Think about anything but that.
Think about ... it doesn't matter. Something else. Anything else!

~

The group of Sadducees passed by me outside the temple, intent on something or another. The Pharisees had left a little earlier, storming out and mumbling curses about Jesus, and now a group of Sadducees were headed into the temple with the same determined air. Curiosity drove me after them, right into the temple.

These Sadducees were at odds with all the other upper-crust folks because they didn't believe that God was going to resurrect the dead. They said all we had was the here and now.

I'm not sure why I cared. I suppose a part of me also just wanted to believe in the resurrection, the idea that there was something more than ... this. If the Sadducees were right, then what advantage do the "righteous" have over the "wicked"? Ultimately, they both lie just as peacefully in the grave.

The Sadducees believed in a version of God that was like having no God at all. But they would still look down their noses at the people I knew who, behind closed doors, had admitted to me that they weren't sure God cared at all or even existed. They would just as soon stone such people as look at them, but were their beliefs any different?

They approached Jesus.

"*Teacher*," said the leader, his purpose belied by a hint of over-eagerness, "we have a question for you."[127]

Jesus turned to them.

"Moses said that if a man dies without having children, his brother should marry his wife and have children for him. Suppose there were seven brothers. The first married a woman, but died young with no children. Then the second married her, but he also died childless. In fact, all seven brothers died without having children. Finally, the woman died as well.

"Now, when the supposed resurrection comes, whose wife will she

---

[127] Matthew 22:23-33, Mark 12:18-27, Luke 20:27-40

be? All seven were married to her, after all."

Jesus responded. "You have made a grave mistake because you do not understand the Scriptures and you do not understand God's power. At the resurrection, people will neither be married nor given in marriage. They will be like the angels in heaven. And if you question the resurrection and God's power, consider this: long after their death, God said, 'I am the God of Abraham, the God of Isaac, and the God of Jacob.'"

Jesus turned away from the Sadducees and addressed everyone nearby, all of whom were already listening anyway.

"Friends! He's not the God of the dead but of the living!"

A mumble of confusion and amazement moved through the crowd. Some looked astounded, others looked confused or even angry.

I didn't understand it.

As another man began to question Jesus, I made my way outside.

Not the God of the dead, but of the living? But they *are* dead! I thought they were supposed to come back like later or something. What is he saying, that they're alive *right now*, walking around with angels or something?

~

Resurrection is a comforting thought when you are dying. How nice it would be for someone in my situation to know that, as miserable and painful and nearly unbearable as this is, when it's over all that remains is heaven.

I'm pretty sure heaven's not for the likes of me, though.

~

Barrabbas stood just at the edge of the corner, watching the lone Roman soldier.

He whispered to Jaap and me, "Just a few more seconds."

No! Please! Think about something else! Anything else!

~

"Just hold one more moment," said Barabbas. "Wait for my signal."

The soldier drew closer. I remember every detail of those seconds. Time seemed to move in slow motion.

He turned so that his back was to us. Barabbas gave the signal.

~

I'm crying now. I can't stop it. Why must this moment play in my head over and over? Is my suffering on this cross not enough?

~

We were on him before he knew what was happening.

Barabbas stabbed, again and again, again and again. The soldier hit the ground.

"Good, nice and quiet," said Barabbas, not the least bit concerned at what he'd done. He was always like that. "Now, let's move in to—"

"What are you doing?! No!" The voice came from behind us. A man was running up, but he wasn't another Roman soldier.

He was a Jew, like us.

"Quiet, man!" whispered Barabbas harshly. "Don't make so much noise!"

"You must stop! You'll bring down the Romans on us all!" His voice hadn't quieted in the least.

"Shut up, I said!" Barabbas brandished the knife. "This doesn't concern you. Just get out of here, pretend you didn't see *anything*!"

"He's still breathing! Just leave him alone, maybe he'll be okay! He didn't even see you! Just leave!"

"This is your last warning!" Barabbas realized that his voice was becoming louder and quieted again to a whisper. "We don't have time for this. We've got to keep moving or we'll miss the rendezvous with the others."

"I'm sorry," said the man. "I can't let you do this."

He moved to run but I grabbed his arm.

He eyes looked into mine. They were filled with fear.

I used my knife. I ... it was so terrible. I thought I wasn't this person.

He fell ...

What have I done?

The rest of that day went by like a dream. Barabbas urged me to keep going and I numbly followed. Our little ragtag group—even joined by many others—trying to revolt against the might of the Roman army ... it was utterly pointless. We were soon in retreat. The few of us who made it out that day counted ourselves lucky to escape with our lives. But for weeks afterwards the Romans hunted for Barabbas and anyone associated with him, until they finally found us.

Every night since that day I see the face of the innocent Jewish man I killed. In the daytime I can usually put him out of my mind. But at night, he torments my dreams.

~

The tears are flowing freely now. I can't stop them. Even so, no one seems concerned. I'm just another criminal dying on a cross.

No, heaven isn't for me. I can never be forgiven.

Looking back on my life now, I see that it wasn't just that one event. I'm not a man who's tried to love God and tried to love his neighbors, but has fallen short. That moment was only the culmination of a life of violence, theft, cruelty, and selfishness.

I'm on this cross because I deserve to be on this cross. And now I'm going to die. Even if someone were to rescue me right now and bring me down from here, I'd still soon die from my wounds. I am utterly and completely without hope. I deserve every drop of blood and tears.

It occurs to me that, while I deserve to be here and Jaap deserves to be here, so does Barabbas. I don't know where he is. But here, in his place, is this man Jesus. They can't even figure out what to charge him with, but they are killing him anyway. He suffers the same fate as me. How is that right?

I turn towards him and I'm surprised to see he's already staring at me. He must be the only person here who cares that I am crying. He has that look again, determined compassion, as if even while he suffers just as I do—his suffering made all the worse by his innocence—he still has room to empathize with me. But there's something else too. It's like he's, I don't know ... waiting.

But waiting for what? What does he want from me?

One of the newcomers in the crowd begins taking up the same mocking comments Jesus has been enduring all morning.

"Hey!" he says. "I thought you were the *Messiah*! Can't you just come down from there? Don't you have some followers who can fight for you or something?"

Jesus doesn't respond. He's still staring at me.

He should be angry. Anyone else would be angry. He doesn't deserve to be up here. And who mocks a man like this as he's suffering and dying?

"Some Messiah. You all saw those things he did. He healed all those people. He even raised Lazarus from the dead! Now he's going to die like everyone else. Us Jews really are a pathetic people, eh? Even our *Messiah* can't do anything against these Romans."

The man spits on the ground and walks away.

But what ... hold on ... what was it he said? He's going to die? He's going to die? He even raised Lazarus from the dead?

He's going to die.

He raised Lazarus from the dead.

The words from his conversation now flash in my mind: He is not the God of the dead but of the living.

Abraham, Isaac, and Jacob, they died, but they're alive somewhere. Death isn't a problem for God.

Lazarus died, but he's alive. Death isn't a problem for Jesus.

Jesus is going to die.

Death isn't a problem for Jesus.

So—

My thoughts are interrupted by a cry from Jaap from his cross on the other side of Jesus. He must have moved and hurt something. He begins cursing and screaming in a fit of rage.

When he calms down a little, he directs his anger at Jesus. "Come on, *Messiah*, why not save yourself and get down from there! Maybe you can save us too while you're at it!"[128]

"Jaap!" I yell, anger bubbling up within me. "Don't you fear God, even when you are about to die? We deserve to be on this cross, we deserve everything we are getting and even more, for the wrong we've done! But what has this man done? Nothing! They couldn't even think of something to charge him with!"

Jesus hasn't taken his eyes off of me.

Do I dare? But what have I got to lose?

"Jesus," I say, hesitantly, "remember me when you come into your kingdom."

Jesus smiles at me. "I promise you, today you will be with me in paradise!"

I'm vaguely aware that Jaap begins laughing, but I'm not really listening to him.

Paradise. Today. Could it really be true? Jesus, Abraham, Isaac, Jacob and ... *me*?

I'm thinking about this for some time amidst my pain and labored breaths. I notice Jesus again. Now his face is turned forward. He almost looks expectant—whoa. What just happened? Am I okay?

Everything is suddenly dimmer. I can see, but it's like it was suddenly late evening or early morning. I don't remember anyone saying the cross messes up your eyes. What's happening?

My eyes slowly adjust until I can make out what's going on around me.

It's not just me. The crowd of onlookers is huddling closer together and mumbling fearfully amongst themselves. The mockers are utterly silent.

---

[128] Luke 23:39-43

Soon people start talking openly again. They are saying it's not a cloud, they can still see the sun. They are asking each other what's going on. Some of them question Jesus—this time with a much more respectful tone, I notice—but he gives no reply.

The centurion and soldiers guarding us are no longer sitting but are on their feet. They seem completely at a loss. The centurion keeps glancing up at Jesus and mumbling something that I can't hear.

Many of the crowd leave, perhaps to find their families or see if they can find out what's going on.

The sun remains dark and no one knows why.

A few minutes pass and nothing more happens. The novelty of the dim sun begins to wear off and I'm again alone with my pain, trying desperately to distract myself.

I try to remember details about my childhood. I try to remember the good times. I try desperately not to think about the events that got me here, but they keep coming back anyway. And Jesus' words run through my mind again and again: "Today you will be with me in paradise."

Time marches on, but so much more slowly than normal, as if even time wants to watch my suffering for a while before moving on. I feel like I've been up here struggling for breath and trying to ignore the pain for days, but I know it's only been hours.

In the darkness much of the crowd persists, though the attitude has changed entirely. No one dares mock anymore. Those that remain seem to be waiting for something else to happen. But, for a few hours, nothing does.

It's well into the afternoon now. Just as suddenly as it dimmed, and with the same lack of warning, the sun brightens.

Everyone waits expectantly for something to happen. They don't have to wait long.

"My God, my God, why have you forsaken me?"[129] says Jesus in a loud voice. It's the first time he's spoken since the darkness started.

But what's he saying? Why would he suddenly think God … wait … hold on, I've heard that before.

---

[129] Matthew 27:46-49, Mark 15:33-36

A man in the crowd turns to the others. "I bet he's calling for Elijah or something!"

Elijah? I don't think that's right. Something is nagging at me. That phrase, my God, my God, why have you forsaken me … it's familiar. I know it.

Jesus looks at a few in the crowd. "I'm thirsty,"[130] he says, calmly. One of them runs off to get something to drink.

I'm still thinking about that phrase … ah! I know what it is. It's that song, one of those from David.[131] How did it go? I can't remember all of it, but parts are coming back to me. I remember, "Dogs surround me, a pack of villains encircles me. They pierce my hands and my feet. All my bones are on display. People stare and gloat over me." It sounds exactly like what is happening to Jesus right now. Did this happen to David too or something? I don't think anyone ever pierced David's hands and feet. So, was David talking about Jesus, way back in ancient times?

The man who left to get a drink runs back with a sponge on a stick. He raises it up to Jesus' lips and he takes a drink.

"Okay, now leave him alone," says another man. "Let's see if Elijah comes to get him."

When he's finished drinking, Jesus lets out a sigh of relief. It's hard to see, but I think he's smiling. He calls out, "Father, into your hands I commit my spirit![132] *It is finished!*"[133]

He bows his head and dies. But it's not right, it's not like death I've seen which takes you whether you want it to or not. It is like he's choosing to die, right now, at this moment, and death's only option is to obey. Like he decided beforehand, right now is the time—

The ground begins to shake.[134] Fresh shots of pain rack my body as the shaking irritates wounds. I can hear Jaap crying out as well.

I see a boulder nearby and I could swear it *splits in two*.

What is going on?

---

[130] John 19:28-29
[131] Psalm 22
[132] Luke 23:46
[133] Matthew 27:50, Mark 15:37, John 19:30
[134] Matthew 27:51

The shaking ceases and silence reigns as everyone around tries to understand what just happened.

The first to speak is the centurion. His voice is shaking. "I've never seen anyone die like this. Surely this man was innocent! He actually was God's son!"[135]

The soldiers in his command, who were looking to him for some kind of explanation, look terrified.

The crowd begins dispersing, mumbling amongst themselves,[136] but a few stick around. The women who've been mourning for him do not leave, and the men I see standing at a distance linger as well.[137]

I don't understand it. I don't understand any of it. All I can do is trust what he said: "Today you will be with me in paradise." But it's hard with his dead body hanging next to me.

Soon a small group of soldiers arrives. The centurion and other guards are quickly on their feet. One of the newcomers steps before the centurion.

"Pilate says to speed it up," he says. "Only a few hours until sunset and those Jews are complaining about the Sabbath again."

The centurion shrugs and steps aside.[138]

Oh no. No, please no!

Another soldier, brandishing an iron club steps forward.

No no no. No. I don't think I can do this. Please, no.

He approaches Jaap, whose words echo my thoughts.

"Whoa, come on man. No! Just hold on. Wait just a second—" the iron club is brought down hard against his legs. I can't see him, but I hear shattering of bone. He shouts briefly but then makes no other noise.

He's over there suffocating. I'm next. *Please no! No, please no!*

The soldier moves towards Jesus.

"No," says the centurion. "That one's dead."

"What?" asks the soldier. "Already? He's not faking or something?"

"He's not faking."

---

[135] Matthew 27:54, Mark 15:39, Luke 23:47
[136] Luke 23:48
[137] Matthew 27:55-56, Mark 15:40-41, Luke 23:49
[138] John 19:31-37

"Look, man, Pilate is going to want us to be sure."

The centurion lets out a disgusted sigh. Turning to one of his soldiers, he signals, and the man hands him his spear.

"No need to go around breaking dead bodies for no reason," says the centurion. "Look." He stabs the spear into Jesus side and immediately blood and water flow from his body.

"What was *that*?" asks the soldier, staring at the outpouring of liquid.

"You get that sometimes," is all the centurion said in reply.

The soldier grunts acknowledgement.

Now he walks towards me, iron club in hand.

No. No no no.

"No, please! Please don't!"

He doesn't respond. It doesn't even seem to register that I'm talking.

"Please stop! Stop! *No*! Just ... just ... just ... wait, just wait, don't—"

Aaahhhhh!

The pain is ... the pain ...

I can't breathe! I can't breathe! I can't ...

The pain ...

...

Just think about ... just think about something el—it hurts!

I can't breathe!

I can't ... it's ...

I can't ...

I ...

It hurts! I can't stand it! It hurts!

I can't breathe!

I can't ...

I can't ...

I ...

...

Jesus ...

...

...

...

It's gone. The pain is gone. What's happening?

I'm breathing easily. I can move my arms and legs. I've never felt so good. I feel strong, healthy, and whole. It's like my body is finally what it was supposed to be.

I open my eyes.

It's so beautiful! *He's* so beautiful!

I'm not worthy of this, after all I've done, I don't deserve—

"Well done, my good and faithful servant!"[139]

---

[139] Matthew 25:14-30

Faithful

Boaz could only watch as his cousin Elimelech placed the last of the bags on the last of the donkeys.[140] He saw Elimelech's wife, Naomi, standing nearby. Even at her age, she was an absolutely beautiful woman. She had one arm around each of their two sons, both now at least a foot taller than her.[141]

Elimelech sighed an anxious but hopeful sigh, turning to his wife for comfort. She gave him a pleasant smile, then said to her sons, "It's time. Are you ready for our adventure?" They shrugged unenthusiastically.

Boaz knew that she must be feeling the same anxiousness as her husband, but she didn't show it. That was how she always was. Naomi means "pleasant," and Boaz had never met someone who was so aptly named.

Boaz was just one among the crowd of people who'd come to see them off. It seemed like half the men in Bethlehem—and nearly all of the women—were there to say goodbye.

Most of the women were crying. There were few that Naomi hadn't blessed at one time or another.

Most of the men were silent and anxious, lost in contemplation about whether they, too, should move themselves and their family away to escape the famine. It seemed that for years the harvests had been getting smaller with no end in sight.

Naomi brought two donkeys over for her sons, but before they could mount she hugged them again. "Don't worry!" she said. "The Moabites are our relatives. We'll be treated well there."

In a failed attempt at relaxed joviality, their father contributed, "And I hear the girls are very pretty!"

"Yes," said Naomi in muffled tones as she continued hugging them tightly, "in a few years it will be time to find wives for you!"

The two blushed but noticeably brightened up at this prospect.

---

[140] Ruth 2:1, Ruth 2:3, Ruth 2:20, Ruth 3:12; At least one man was more closely related to Elimelech than Boaz, so it's likely Boaz was his cousin.
[141] Ruth 1:1-2

Naomi released her embrace and smiled again at them. The two sons mounted their donkeys and Naomi did as well.

Elimelech turned to the crowd who'd come to see them off and smiled nervously.

Boaz stepped forward and hugged Elimelech. Then he pulled him aside to talk out of earshot of everyone else.

"Don't go, cousin," said Boaz. "Just trust in Yahweh. He'll protect us from this famine and the blessings will come again soon. You just need to wait a little longer."

"Boaz," said Elimelech, "you don't know what it's like. You don't have a wife or kids to look after. How can I watch my children waste away? Watch them starve to death?"

Boaz replied, "Look around! Look at all these people; see how much they love you. You and Naomi have done so much for so many. Any of them would happily help you! I myself would die of starvation before I would see your children go hungry!"

"Boaz, it's done. The bags are packed. I've already sold my land."

"Then redeem it! You know it's your right! God's law says that land is yours, others can only buy the rights to use it until the Year of Jubilee, and you can buy it back at a fair price whenever you want.[142] The only thing you stand to lose is a little pride."

Elimelech sighed and gave Boaz a hopeless look.

"Listen," Boaz continued, "let me buy it for you. I'm your family, so I have the same rights to redeem it as you. They can't legally refuse me. God did not want all of the land being gobbled up by a handful of rich people, he wanted every family to have their own."

"Boaz—"

"And, as you've said, I have no family. My wife is dead, I have no children, but I don't lack for possessions! It seems that my whole life God has thwarted every chance I had at a family, but he's given me more money than I know what to do with. Perhaps he's done that exactly for times like this. Let me redeem the land for you. And stay!"

"No, Boaz. No. I can still take care of my family. It wouldn't be right for me to use what belongs to you."

---

[142] Leviticus 25:8-55

Boaz looked hopelessly at his cousin. Then he sighed, smiled, and hugged him again.

"Then be safe, and I hope to see you again someday," said Boaz, with genuine feeling. They hugged once more, and then Elimelech said his goodbyes and started off.

~

Years passed. The famine grew worse. Boaz gave to friends and neighbors and anyone else in need. Entire families were only able to survive because of his generosity, yet he himself never went without. Every time he gave it seemed God would replace what he'd given and then some.

Eventually, the famine ended and the harvests became plentiful again. Boaz's wealth grew even more. His fields produced enough crops to support him and his many workers with an abundance left over. It seemed that God had filled to overflowing everything in his life. Everything, that is, except a family. He was still alone and growing older.

He prayed and beseeched God, desperately asking for a wife and at least one son; someone to be an heir to everything God had given him. But as time wore on, and God's silence continued, his hope faded, until it was no more.

~

Ten years after his cousin had departed for Moab, Boaz received word of Naomi's return.[143]

It was in late spring, very early in the barley harvest. He had gone out of Bethlehem and into his fields to check on his workers. When he saw them, he gave the greeting he always did. "Yahweh be with you!" he called out to them.[144]

---

[143] Ruth 1:4-6
[144] Ruth 2:4

And they gave the same reply they always did. "Yahweh bless you!"

Boaz's foreman, Asher, stepped forward and greeted him. Boaz detected a hint of over eagerness.

"How goes it?" asked Boaz.

"Everyone's healthy," said Asher. "The new guys are working out well so far."

"And how about you?"

"My wife is doing well after the birth, and baby Joash is growing stronger every day. I think he's going to be fine."

"Good, good."

"Did you hear about Naomi?" asked Asher.

It took Boaz a moment to adjust to this sudden change in topic, and a further moment to search his mind for anyone named Naomi he could think of other than his cousin's wife whom he'd seen leave so many years ago. "Naomi?" he asked, finally.

"Yes," said Asher. "*That* Naomi, who was Elimelech's wife. One of the workers told me she came into town quietly last night. Not many people know yet, but I'm sure by tonight it will be all anyone's talking about. Women *still* talk about the nice things she did for them."

Boaz, trying to process all of this, picked up on a phrase. "*Was* Elimelech's wife? He's dead?"

"Yes, he died in Moab, apparently not too long after they got there.[145] I'm sorry. I know he was like a brother to you."

Boaz sat down on the ground. His head was swimming with too many thoughts and emotions that he wasn't yet sure what to do with. Asher sat next to him.

"Sir," said Asher, using a formal tone that immediately made Boaz weary that more bad news was coming, "I'm afraid it's worse. His two sons are dead too. They married, but they died before having any children. She has no husband, no sons, no descendants at all."[146]

Boaz let out a long, sorrowful sigh. "She's lost everything. Poor Naomi."

"She said not to call her that anymore," said Asher. "She said to call

---

[145] Ruth 1:3
[146] Ruth 1:4-5

her 'Mara', since God has made her bitter."[147]

"I can't imagine her being anything other than Naomi," said Boaz. Mara means "bitter", a stark contrast to "pleasant", but from what Boaz remembered of the woman, even in her bitterness she was probably focused on helping people around her.

"Yeah, you're right about that." Asher paused. "The worker said she's still a lovely woman, even at her age," he said, with a hint of suggestion in his voice.

"Very subtle," said Boaz, as he glared at his foreman. "Don't you think it's a little soon to be telling me to marry my dead cousin's wife?"

"Maybe for you," replied the foreman. "You just heard about it. But for her, he's been dead for years. You know you are one of their family redeemers. Your cousin sold the land when they left. Naomi has the right to redeem it as long as she pays the cost but there's no way she could ever afford that, and now she has no sons to inherit it. The poor woman is left with nothing. The person who bought the land may not have to give it back in the Year of Jubilee, because there may be no one to give it back *to*."

"So," said Boaz, "I should do what? Buy back the land and redeem it for her? Marry her? Have a son to inherit it?[148] It won't work, Asher. She's too old to have any more children, and I have none either. Both of our inheritance's are lost, no matter what I do."

"Well, sir," said Asher, and again Boaz noted the formality, "there is another."

Boaz gave Asher a confused look.

Asher continued. "As I said, while they were there, in Moab, Elimelech's sons both married, though they didn't have children. One of their widows came back with Naomi. Her name is Ruth. She refused to leave Naomi's side. She said she wanted to be one of our people and to serve Yahweh."[149]

Boaz thought for a moment. "This Ruth ... she followed Naomi here? She stuck by Naomi's side even after everything that happened to her, even though it meant moving to a foreign land and a people she

---

[147] Ruth 1:20-21
[148] Deuteronomy 25:5-10
[149] Ruth 1:6-19

doesn't know?"

"Yes," said Asher. "And *she* is certainly young enough to have children. Perhaps it's not too late for you to have a wife and a family of your own?"

"That's enough, Asher." Boaz stood up and dusted himself off. "I'm not going to force some young woman to marry a used-up old man like me. Elimelech has a nephew who's still single, and I hear he's doing well for himself. Let him redeem the land and marry Naomi's daughter-in-law. He's a closer relative so he has first right before me anyway.[150] Then they can have a son who will inherit the land, and Naomi's family won't lose it."

"Yes, sir," was all the foreman replied, but his expression belied his concern for his master. He went back and joined the rest of the workers in harvesting the barley.

Over the next few days Boaz went about his business like normal, and since it was harvest time there was plenty of business to go about. The exception to his normal routine was that he spent a little extra time listening to any news of Naomi's return that he could pick up on. The woman was completely heartbroken, saying that God had sent her away full but brought her back empty.

He also heard stories of Ruth. Everyone who met her spoke highly of her, saying she was kind and diligent and truly cared for Naomi.

For all his curiosity, Boaz was careful not to come by and visit. Elimelech's nephew, as the closest relative, should be taking care of this situation. Boaz didn't want to interfere with that or give anyone the impression that he was greedily grabbing up a chance at more land or a young wife.

Try as he might to keep his routine, he was having trouble sleeping. The next few nights were spent weeping tears no one saw before finally falling asleep. He'd been pleading with God for so long for a wife and a family. Years and even decades had gone by with no reply. Opportunities came and then fell through one way or another. He tried to trust in God despite the silence. Eventually, the only way he knew to dull the pain was to put it out of his mind and not think about it. Now,

---

[150] Ruth 3:12

with Naomi's return and Asher's hint that he should go after this young woman Ruth, hope threatened to spring back again, and with it came the pain, and with the pain came the tears.

A few days after Naomi's return, he went out again to his field. As he approached his workers to greet them, he noticed someone new; a beggar of some kind. She was following behind the other women who were gleaning what the harvesters had missed and picking up any barley that was still left behind.

"Yahweh be with you!" he called out to his workers.

"Yahweh bless you!" they responded.

As Asher approached, Boaz asked, "Who does that young woman belong to?"[151]

"*That*," said his foreman, in a tone that was in the running for the world anti-subtlety award, "is Ruth, the Moabite daughter-in-law of Naomi. She asked me if she could glean behind the workers today. She's a hard worker too. She's been doing it all morning, except for one short rest in the shelter."

"Hrm ... So, Ruth and Noami are reduced to begging now?"

"Yes," said Asher. "It's a shame too, because she's a foreigner. She's not even an Israelite and has barely any protection at all. I guess this nephew of Elimelech's, this *family redeemer* who's supposed to be taking care of them really isn't doing such a great job, eh? If only there was someone else in the family, some other *family redeemer*, who could step in and help ..."

Boaz glared at Asher. The younger man smiled, winked, and returned to his work.

Boaz approached Ruth.[152] She noticed him and stood nervously to attention.

She probably figured out I'm the owner and is afraid that I'm going to kick her out, thought Boaz.

But shortly her expression morphed into a nervous smile, returning the one Boaz didn't realize was on his on face.

"Greetings Ruth, daughter-in-law of Naomi," he said.

"Sir," she responded with a slight bow of her head. She glanced in

---

[151] Ruth 2:3-7
[152] Ruth 2:8-13

the direction of Asher, hoping for some validation that she wasn't about to be mistreated or sent away.

"Listen," said Boaz, "it's okay. It's good that you've come to my field and not somewhere else. You'll be safe here. I'll tell the men not to lay a hand on you. In fact, you should stay here throughout the harvest. Work behind the women and glean what you can for you and Naomi. And feel free to use the water the men have to get a drink whenever you are thirsty."

Ruth fell down to her knees and then bowed until her face touched the ground in a show of absolute gratitude. "What makes you treat me so kindly, sir? You know I'm only a foreigner."

"I also know what you've done for Naomi. You left your family and your people to stay by her side with no guarantee of food or safety. Now you've come into the land of Israel, under the protection of Yahweh, and may he richly reward you for all the kindness you've shown to Naomi."

"Thank you, sir. I was so nervous to be out here working in a field that I had no right to be in. You've put me at ease. I hope I continue to find favor in your eyes."

Boaz smiled brightly at Ruth, and then turned back towards his workers just in time to see another wink from Asher. He approached him and the other workers.

Boaz spent the rest of the morning harvesting in the field alongside his workers, trying his hardest to subdue his tumultuous inner thoughts. He told himself that he should just stop thinking about it and focus on the work, but Hope refused to die. *You think God wants you to be alone*, it said. *But you don't know that. You don't know the mind of Yahweh; you have no idea what he could be planning. He's good and kind and surprising. You've seen it a hundred times. This might have been his plan all along.*

And look at her. She's attractive, isn't she? On top of it all—kind, noble, hard-working, humble, caring, wise—she's also beautiful. It almost seems unfair that a woman should possess all those qualities and *be beautiful. And now it seems you might have a chance at the pleasure of a wife and family. If you have at least two sons, then both your family line and Naomi's will continue. Maybe, just maybe, after all these years God will finally fulfill your plea. Maybe you won't be alone anymore.*

Bitterness also attempted to step in to crush Hope, telling him that if God really cared about him he would have never put him through this in the first place, but Boaz had long ago learned to recognize that treacherous inner voice. He silenced it immediately. He didn't know if he could trust in Hope, but nevertheless Bitterness had to die. In his emotional state the only thing he knew for sure he could trust was that which he'd already mentally solidified years ago: God is good and cares for his people.

At mealtime he called Ruth over to eat the roasted grain with himself and the rest of his workers.[153] Again, she seemed exceedingly grateful. She ate quickly and left to get back to gleaning even before any of his workers had finished.

Once she had gotten up, Boaz told his workers, "Listen, treat her well. None of you are to give her a hard time. Let her gather as much as she wants and don't reprimand her. In fact, I want you to 'accidentally' drop a few for her."

Asher, in typical fashion, was the first to respond and did so with a big smile. "Sure thing. You're the boss!"

When evening approached, Boaz and the workers began threshing the grain they had harvested, and Ruth did the same. It was late in the day when she finally gathered up her barley grain—Boaz happily noted it was quite a large amount—and went home to Naomi.[154]

The next day, Ruth did the same thing, following behind the women gleaning in the day and threshing in the evening. She also did the same the day after and the day after that. She worked hard in the fields every day through the entire barley harvest in late spring and into the wheat harvest in early summer.[155]

Boaz was also busy with the harvest, though his thoughts were increasingly consumed with Ruth. She worked so diligently every day, slaving through the hot sun for enough food for her and Naomi. He wanted to do more for her, but he knew things would be better for her if Elimelech's nephew took care of her and Naomi, as was his

---

[153] Ruth 2:14-16
[154] Ruth 2:17-18
[155] Ruth 2:23

responsibility. He found himself growing angry at this nephew of Elimelech who seemed oblivious to their plight and did nothing about it. If this continued on much longer, Boaz would have to confront him. He was already thinking about what he would say, how he could play it just right so that no matter what happened Naomi and Ruth were taken care of.

One night, after a long day of work and an evening spent threshing, Boaz went to sleep near the threshing floor as was his habit and that of many of the workers during the days of the harvest. In the middle of the night, he suddenly awoke after having bumped his foot on something he didn't expect.

His feet were freezing. Why were they uncovered? And where was that perfume smell coming from? And what had he just bumped with his foot?

In the dim light he could just barely make out a figure, lying down near his foot.

"Who are you?" he whispered.

"I am your servant Ruth," replied the figure. "Spread your blanket over me, for you are my family redeemer."[156]

Oh ... oh! thought Boaz, now suddenly very awake. *A beautiful young woman is right here, asking to share a bed with me. I've been alone so long. It's late. Everyone else is asleep. No one would see ...*

Temptation lured its ugly head, but like Bitterness, Boaz was well acquainted with its tricks and lies. *No*, he thought. *Trust God, do things his way, he'll bless you for it ...*

After gathering himself, Boaz said, "How kind and loyal you are to Naomi. You could have gone after some other man, someone rich or young or both, but to make sure she is taken care of and your family has an inheritance, you've come to me. You are a virtuous woman. Please don't worry about a thing, I will take care of this. But you should know that, while I am one of your family redeemers, there is another man more closely related than I. I must speak to him first and get this matter settled. If he is willing to redeem your land and marry you, then good. But if not, I will marry you, and Yahweh who protects you has

---

[156] Ruth 3:7-15

heard me say it. Now, stay here until morning but get up early so no one sees that you were here."

There was no more sleep to be had for Boaz that night. He thought about how to get Ruth out of there in the morning without anyone seeing. He thought about how to approach Elimelech's nephew, playing the conversation out in his head over and over again. He tried desperately not to think about Ruth, lying nearby, whose embrace may very soon finally put an end his years of loneliness ... unless this other man should marry her.

In the morning he sent her off early, before it was light enough to see, with a large amount of grain so that she wouldn't return to Naomi empty-handed. Then he went into town and sat at the city gate, among the other leaders who could act as witnesses, and waited for the nephew.

He'd been rehearsing this moment in his head all night. Boaz would either convince the man to marry Ruth and make sure Elimelech's family had an inheritance, or he would convince him to publicly agree not to do it and allow Boaz to. He mentally pleaded with God that it would be the latter.

He didn't have to wait long before the man was heading to go out through the city gate.[157] He called him over. "Friend, come over here and sit down, I have business I need to discuss with you."

The man came over and sat down. The older men around the gate began listening, as usual, so that any transactions would have public witnesses.

Here we go, thought Boaz.

"I need to talk to you about Naomi's land. Someone needs to redeem it for her, since both her husband and sons are dead. I am willing to redeem it, but I wanted to speak to you first because you are first in line to do it."

Boaz could almost see the wheels spinning in the man's head. Redeeming a land with no heirs to it ... there's no one to take care of it, so naturally it would be up to him to take care of it. It would effectively become his. And when the Year of Jubilee comes, when he would

---

[157] Ruth 4:1-12

normally need to return it to the owner, there would be no one to return it to. This land would become his family's *forever*. Elimelech's family's loss would become his family's gain.

"All right, I'll redeem it," said the man, a little too eagerly.

Phase one complete, thought Boaz.

"Of course," said Boaz, with a glance to the bystanders to remind the man that there were witnesses, "it wouldn't be right for you to redeem the land and not provide an heir. It would need to eventually be returned to Elimelech's family, so you would have to marry Ruth and father a son for their family, as the law requires. Your first son would belong to their family, but any other sons would be yours."

The man looked around apprehensively. Again, Boaz could almost hear his thoughts. What if he only had one son? Then Elimelech's land would be safe, but his would be lost. He'd be in the same situation as Naomi's family.

"Then ... I can't redeem it," he said. "That would endanger my own inheritance." He removed his sandal, a sign known in Bethlehem at the time to mean the deal was finalized, and held it out to Boaz. "You buy the land, and you marry Ruth, because I cannot."

It worked, thought Boaz. *It actually worked!*

He took the sandal with a smile. Then he turned to the surrounding witnesses. "You are all here today witnessing that I am buying Elimelech's land. And with that land, I will marry Ruth, the Moabite widow, so that she can have a son to carry on Elimelech's family name and inherit his land. You have all witnessed this today."

Many of those around were the leaders of the town, older men who had known Boaz much of his life and seen the heartbreak as he endured years with no family. They made no attempt to contain their joy.

One man, who was particularly excited for Boaz, decided he'd be the spokesperson. "We are witnesses," he said with a smile. "And may this woman coming into your house be like Rachel and Leah, the mothers of all Israel. May Yahweh bless you with many children!"

That very day, Boaz married Ruth and took her home as his wife. Almost immediately they conceived, and soon after she gave birth to a son for Naomi's family. Naomi adopted the child as her own and named him Obed. She raised him, and her family's land finally had someone to inherit it.[158]

Boaz and Ruth had more children afterward for their own family. His obedience to God led to salvation for two widows and the protection of someone else's land from being gobbled up by greedy neighbors. And the blessings weren't only for others. He was also finally given the desire of his heart—a wife and a family—long after it felt impossible that anything like that should happen. And his own land and inheritance was protected as well.

Possibly most important of all, the actions of this normal man leading a faithful life, were of tremendous historical significance, because Obed would one day become a father himself to a son named Jesse, who would in turn become a father to David, who would be the greatest king Israel ever knew and would point to an even greater king among his own descendants, *the* king and savior of the world: Jesus.[159]

And so, even now, three thousand years later, the story of this normal man acting faithfully is told around the world.

---

[158] Ruth 4:13-17
[159] Ruth 4:18-22, Matthew 1:5-16

The Unlikely Angel

In the bright and glorious court of the Most High, the angels of heaven assembled. A countless throng surrounded the throne, attending the one on it, who shone as bright as the sun. The angels stood on a flat surface as smooth as glass and clear as crystal that seemed to go on for miles with vibrant colors flowing through it like fire.[160]

At their head, standing in front of the throne and facing the rest of the angels, was the esteemed Gabriel,[161] the messenger of the births of John and Jesus, and bringer of visions to the prophet Daniel. At his side stood Michael,[162] the general and prince of all of heaven's armies, whose skill in battle none could match.

Gabriel raised his hand and the crowd of angels grew silent. He spoke, and his voice carried with unworldly effectiveness to all he addressed.

"As all of you know, this is a difficult time for the humans. Many have been scattered from their homes, and the persecution in the country of Judea is growing.[163] That scoundrel King Herod has even arrested and killed our King's beloved friend, James, and now he has arrested Peter, intending to do the same for him.[164] Roman soldiers guard Peter day and night, but the prayers of those who love him have been heard. God has caused these events to be set in motion and decreed that the humans must wait patiently and continue their prayer.

"But now it is time to act! God has ordered that we rescue Peter from prison and finally put an end to Herod and his schemes. I have asked God's permission to perform this mission myself, but he refused. Instead, he wishes for a volunteer from among you.

"So, who will go? Who will rescue Peter from prison and the humans' intended execution and finally give Herod the death he

---

[160] Revelation 4:6, Revelation 15:2
[161] Daniel 8:16, Daniel 9:21, Luke 1:19, Luke 1:26
[162] Daniel 10:13, Daniel 10:21, Daniel 12:1, Jude 1:9, Revelation 12:7
[163] Acts 8:1-3, Acts 12:1
[164] Acts 12:2-5

deserves?"

Silence reigned in the court, but only for a moment. Then, an angel stepped forward.

"I volunteer!" The deep bass tones could be felt almost as easily as they were heard. The angel that stepped forward stood taller than all around him. "I, Masheet, champion of Michael himself, volunteer to carry out this mission, as I carried out the mission to rescue God's people from Egypt and so many others.[165] Using the power over nature and material things that God has entrusted with me, I will bring a mighty earthquake to release Peter from his chains and terrify all those who hear about it. None will even dare try to stop him as he simply walks out of the prison, in full view of the guards. Then I will turn towards Herod and bring him a swift and public death. As he has placed himself above those around him, so I will place him below the lowest of low, and lowly worms that dig in the dirt will make a meal of his lifeless body."

A general murmur of approval went through the entire assembly. Gabriel opened his mouth to voice acceptance, but before he could utter a sound another angel spoke.

"I also volunteer!" The graceful figure stepped forward. His voice was as smooth as liquid velvet and he moved with the grace and subtlety of a dancer. "I, Vox, volunteer to carry out this mission. Just as I set a trap for Sisera—so that he slept silently, finally believing he was safe, just before Jael drove a tent peg through his temple[166]—so I will set a trap for Herod, using the power of subtle persuasion that God has granted me. His subjects will tell him what he wants to hear, even comparing him to God, and in doing so will ensure his destruction when he accepts their praise, as a man like him surely will. As soon as he accepts their praise as if he was God, I will put an immediate end to him in front of them all. Peter's trouble will be erased in an instant. He will be released without opposition, and all who hear about it will glorify God."

There was another general murmur of approval, and raised voices as the angels discussed which of the two accomplished individuals

---

[165] Exodus 7 – Exodus 12
[166] Judges 4

would make the better choice.

Gabriel spoke again. "Excellent, excellent. Either of you would make a fine—"

"Me too," said a voice, which contained neither deep bass tones nor smooth and subtle grace, but rather was light and pleasant and, by the standards of the two who'd already volunteered, rather boring.

The angel stepped forward. He appeared neither strong, nor smart, nor terribly impressive in any other way. A permanent, friendly smile was on his face, and it seemed ready to break into a laugh at any second.

"Harvey?" said Gabriel. "From that thing with Balaam?[167] I'm not sure talking donkeys are the solution here, friend."

"You've gotta admit, that was pretty memorable!" said Harvey. "You know, they still talk about it down there."

"Yes, yes," said Gabriel, almost dismissively. "But how do you propose to handle this situation?"

"*Well*," said Harvey, "I haven't really thought that through. I thought maybe I'd just wing it."

"*Wing* it?" said Gabriel.

"Yup. I mean, some of that stuff they said sounds pretty good. I like the bit about the worms."

"Harvey, this is a mission of tremendous importance," said Gabriel. "The humans are sure to write it all down and read about it for years. Millennia from now, they will be sitting together studying the testimonies of those who saw these things happening, poring over every detail to pick out every bit of meaning. This is a very serious mission."

Harvey beamed his ready smile. "Don't worry. God doesn't fail!"

Gabriel opened his mouth to speak once again, but was silenced by a voice coming from the throne. The voice defied description but nevertheless an attempt will be made. It contained beautiful notes that would put the most artful soprano and the deepest bass alike to shame. It was at once a perfectly harmonized symphony and a single, clear, soloist's song. It seemed to contain elements of every creature known

---

[167] Numbers 22 – Numbers 25

to the world, of wind and rustling trees, of ocean waves and even, somehow, of the deep silence of places never roamed by man. It was a voice whose power could be felt, not just in the normal sense but in the *soul*. This was a voice with authority that could not be denied. This was a voice that could call forth life from nothing with a single word.

It said, "Send Harvey. I grant him the power of Masheet and Vox. This will be fun!"

The host of assembled angels bowed low in perfect unison.

Gabriel spoke again. "Praise our glorious God, whose wisdom and goodness have no end! Harvey, you have been granted Masheet's power over nature and material things and Vox's power of subtle persuasion. Go forth! Rescue Peter, Jesus' rock, and bring that despicable Herod to a lowly end!"

"Will do, Gabby!" responded Harvey with another smile. Then he turned and headed down to the human world.

~

Harvey approached the prison, situated outside the human city of Jerusalem, well after the sun had set. He instinctively turned himself invisible, a little trick all angels are capable of, and headed for the roof, intending to pass right to it. He stopped short, however, when he caught sight of the two guards outside of the prison.

He briefly considered the two. It would be easy to just pass through everyone silently and invisibly, but he had these new, temporary powers, and it seemed like a great chance to try them out. Masheet's power gave him control over nearly every natural or material thing. He could kill these guards with a word, if he wanted to.

He descended down near a wall out of sight of the two guards, and then, fighting his natural urge not to, became visible again. Then he made himself appear human, another thing all angels can do.

Harvey peered around the corner at the two guards. They looked exactly as they were: two remarkably fragile humans doing their best to appear strong and menacing and not let anyone know how incredibly bored they were. It was all a show with these humans.

Harvey came out from around the corner and walked confidently towards the two men. It wasn't long before they caught sight of him and he had their full attention. They both made their best effort to rise to their full height and glare menacingly. They were pretty good at it. Like most guards, they'd had plenty of practice doing things menacingly.

Harvey smiled, mostly as a friendly gesture but partially because it was funny being threatened by humans.

"Hello!" he said.

"Don't know what you think you're doing, but you'll want to be somewhere else, friend," said one of the guards, menacingly.

"Friend? Thanks, pal! I do intend to be somewhere else very soon, only there's something I wanted to try out first." Harvey reached out with his new power.

The guard drew his sword menacingly.

"This is your last war—"

And then he slouched and slid down the wall in a manner that was not the least bit menacing. He was instantly fast asleep. The second guard had just enough time to show a brief look of confusion before he followed suit.

"Hey, that was cool!" said Harvey. He stepped past the two now thoroughly unmenacing guards and entered the prison, without bothering to do any of those silly human things like open the door.

Once inside, he looked around. The fact that the light of the prison was dim made little difference to Harvey. Soon, he found what he was looking for: a group of four guards sitting at their little table and playing games to pass the time. None of them had noticed him yet.

"Hello!" he said.

The four stared for a brief moment before instantly rising to attention.

"What's this?" said one of them. "Who are you? This some kind of inspection?"

"Inspection?" said Harvey, considering the word. "No, no. It's really not any kind of inspection. Where I come from, the big guy in charge doesn't have much need for inspections. He already knows what's happening. Every now and then we do it for you humans' benefit, like that time with Sodom and Gom—"[168]

"Well, if it's not an inspection, then what is it?" The confusion on the faces of the guards was slowly being replaced with suspicion.

"Oh! I just want to know where Peter is. Can you point me in the direction of his cell?"

"Why?" The suspicion grew further.

"I'm planning to break him out, you see. Oh, and then later I'm going to kill Herod. That's why I was sent, you know." Harvey beamed his relaxed smile again.

The spokesman for the four guards began laughing. It started small but grew louder into the kind of boisterous laugh that those who think they have the upper hand are so inclined to. The other guards couldn't help but do the same. All the while Harvey smiled his easy smile.

"How'd someone dumb like you manage to survive as a thief and assassin?" said the spokesman, once most of the laughing had abated. "You could have told us you were inspecting or something. Maybe we'd have believed you and told you right where to find Peter. Now we're just gonna kill you!"

"Told you I was inspecting?" said Harvey. "You mean, *lie*? That wouldn't have even occurred to me. Oh, that's clever! You humans are so clever! Dishonest, filled with sin, completely unaware of your own condition, fragile and with horribly broken views of the world around you ... but clever!"

Two of the guards drew their swords and approached Harvey. His smile did not waver.

"Before you do that, though," said Harvey, "could you please tell me where to find Peter?"

"Oh, you'll see him soon enough!" said the spokesman as the two sword-wielders grew even closer. "We'll kill you today, and he'll be joining you tomorrow!"

One of the two approaching guards fell, instantly fast asleep. The other took another two steps before he realized he was now approaching alone.

"Please?" said Harvey, his smile widening.

---

[168] Genesis 18:16-21

The closest guard, who'd now stopped approaching, said, "Wha? What'd you do to him?"

"He's fine!" said Harvey. "You'll all be fine. Hmmm ... well, maybe not. I mean, when I let Peter out, Herod is going to be pretty mad. But he'll probably only kill the soldiers who were directly guarding him, so I'm sure none of you have anything to worry about!"[169] Harvey beamed reassurance.

"So," said the spokesman, "what you're sayin' is, either we stop you or Herod might kill us?"

"Yes, I suppose that's true," said Harvey. "He probably won't, but I guess he *might*."

"Well, then," said the spokesman as he, too, drew his sword, "there are still three of us and only one of you. I like those odds better than hoping for mercy from King Herod!"

Two of the three rushed towards Harvey, managing to get in about three steps each before they also stumbled to the ground and began snoring.

Harvey smiled pleasantly at the remaining guard. He was the youngest of the four and had remained quiet to this point. "Can *you* tell me where Peter is?" asked Harvey.

The young guard stood, trembling, and didn't say a word.

"I don't suppose saying 'do not be afraid' will do any good? No? It never does with you humans." Harvey sighed.

He considered his situation for a few seconds; the many corridors of the large prison, the walls, the terrified guard standing before him. Jerusalem was a big city with a big history and had need of large prisons from time-to-time. The prison had spent centuries evolving and changing until it was a massive maze of corridors and cells. It wouldn't be easy to find Peter without the help of *someone*. Masheet's power could put these men to sleep, and could do a whole lot worse should the need arise, but perhaps now was a time to try a different approach.

"Listen," said Harvey. "You're scared, right? A bit creeped out? Not too sure what's going on? That makes sense. I'm a scary angel, after all.

---

[169] Acts 12:18-19

Just be glad I'm not in my normal form!" Harvey laughed. "Oh man, humans *always* freak out when they see us in our normal form. Every time we appear, we have to be all, 'Do not be afraid! Do not be afraid!'[170] It never works though. They always think something bad is about to happen, as if all God does is send angels around to appear to people and tell them bad things! Anyway, how's about you let that fear of yours motivate you to help me out? Just walk me to Peter's cell."

Harvey reached out with Vox's power ...

The quiet man suddenly spoke. "Okay, okay!" he said, now trembling so visibly it almost appeared like a stage act, "I'll take you there! Just please don't do anything to me!"

"Great!" said Harvey with a smile. "Stop a bit short before we get there and just point me the rest of the way."

The guard led Harvey down a series of corridors and stairways until, finally, he stopped a few feet from another corner.

"It's just over there," said the guard at a whisper. "Around that corner and to the right."

"Thanks, pal," said Harvey, also at a whisper. "You've been helpful. Now, you should probably go and see to your friends. And, if I were you guys, I wouldn't go around telling people what I'd seen today. If word gets out you helped Peter escape from Herod, your lives could get a whole lot more miserable, and probably a lot shorter, too."

The guard walked away, slowly and hesitantly at first, but then with greater assurance until soon he was nearly running. Harvey watched him until he was out of sight around a corner. Then he strode confidently towards Peter's cell.

Outside the cell two sentries stood guard. As soon as the sentries spotted him, they grew more alert.

Harvey reached out again with Vox's power. "Hey, you guys aren't aware of me here, okay? Or any of the stuff that I'm about to do. Okay?"

Immediately the two guards relaxed, standing as they were before, as if nothing whatsoever had happened.

Harvey smiled. "Neat! It's like being invisible, except ... I'm not.

---

[170] Genesis 21:17, Judges 6:22-23, Daniel 10:12, Daniel 10:19, Matthew 1:20, Matthew 28:5, Matthew 28:10, Luke 1:13, Luke 1:30, Luke 2:10, Revelation 1:17

They just don't see me."

Harvey approached one and put his hand in front of the sentry's face. There was no reaction. He waved it back and forth. Still no reaction.

"Hey, buddy," he said, at a whisper. The guard stared right through him.

"I said, hey!" said Harvey again, this time louder.

There was still no response.

"So cool …" Harvey smiled to himself. He banged on the cell door. "Oh, no, look, Peter's about to escape. Gosh guys, you better do something!"

Again, the sentries stood perfectly still.

Harvey giggled and passed through the door into the cell. Two guards were chained on either side of Peter,[171] who was sleeping soundly. Both guards were awake and staring at him, having apparently been awakened by his banging on the door.

"Whoops, sorry about that!" said Harvey. "Didn't mean to wake you. You guys should probably just go back to sleep." With another flick of his newfound power the two guards were sleeping peacefully once again.

"Now, for Peter," said Harvey to himself. "Hey, buddy, wake up!"

Peter slumbered softly.

"Hello!" said Harvey, louder. "It's time to go, buddy! I'm getting you out of here!"

Peter shifted slightly, but never opened his eyes.

"Wow, sound sleeper."

Harvey created a light in the cell.

"Wake up, man. Wake up!"

He made the light brighter.

"Time to go. Peter! Peter, wake up!"

He made the light so bright the inside of the cell looked like it was exposed to broad daylight. The effect was disturbing. The lack of cleanliness in the cell was the kind of thing best left in the dark.

"Peter!" Harvey was almost shouting now. "Wake up, Peter!"

---

[171] Acts 12:6

Peter shifted again, but peacefully slumbered on.

"I've heard good things about you, but I gotta admit, I'm a bit impressed! I mean, they were gonna execute you tomorrow and here you are sleeping without a care in the world. That's some real faith. Still ... I really need you to wake up, man."

Harvey sighed. He was not expecting *this* to be the difficult part. More guards on rounds were sure to come by eventually, so if he couldn't get Peter awake soon he would have to deal with them too.

"Welp ... I tried everything else."

Harvey gave Peter a hard kick in the side[172]. "Get *up*, man!"

"Mffrgllr?" said Peter, eloquently.

"Hey, all right! You're awake! Quick, get up!"

With another small blast of Masheet's power the chains were removed from Peter's wrists.

Peter, still dazed, stood up slowly, covering his eyes in the bright light of the cell.

Harvey looked around the room, until he spotted what he was looking for in the corner. "Ah, here we go. Your clothes! Here," he said, handing them to Peter, "put these on."[173]

Peter obeyed.

"Wrap your cloak around you and follow me," said Harvey. "It's a bit chilly outside."

"Outside?" said Peter dreamily, as he wrapped the cloak around him. "This must be some kind of vision."[174]

"Well ... ah, never mind. You'll figure it out soon enough."

Harvey turned towards the door and willed it open, suppressing the urge to say, "Cool!" once again. It might not inspire much confidence in Peter if his angel kept marveling at the things he was able to do.

He led Peter out through the winding paths of the prison, only once needing to use Vox's power to convince a guard that he wasn't seeing anything at all. Peter walked as if in a daze, and kept mumbling to himself about how vivid and real this vision was. Harvey thought about correcting him, but decided it would be a lot more fun to let it

---

[172] Acts 12:7
[173] Acts 12:8
[174] Acts 12:9

play out.

They reached the outside. Harvey led Peter the short distance to the thick, iron gate at the entrance to the city. He opened it using Masheet's power and then closed it after them. He traveled a little further with Peter, turning a corner so they were no longer within site of the gate, and then promptly made himself invisible.[175]

Peter stopped. He stared around him, looking right through Harvey, who, completely unknown to Peter, was laughing wholeheartedly at the entire show.

When the dazed moment had passed, Peter seemed to slowly realize just where he was and just what had happened. His eyes widened, and he actually said, *aloud* (much to Harvey's glee), "Now I know without a doubt that the Lord has sent his angel to rescue me from Herod and from all the Jews were hoping would happen to me!"[176]

Harvey laughed and said, completely unbeknownst to Peter, "Who *talks* like that! Buddy, you're all alone. You're not giving a sermon here."

Peter began walking quickly down the street, a destination clearly in mind. Technically, the first part of Harvey's mission was done, and now all he needed to do was deal with Herod. But he decided to follow Peter to see what happened.

After a few twists and turns down the street, Peter arrived at a house, currently securely locked up for the night but clearly with quite a gathering inside. He knocked on the door.

Harvey passed right inside. He walked further into the house, passing a servant girl who was heading to answer the door, and found a room where many people were gathered. Ah, he thought to himself. This was Mary's house, mother of the young Mark that he had heard so much about.[177] He could see the young man sitting on the floor in the circle with the others. This must be where they were all gathering to pray for Peter's release. Well, they were in for quite a pleasant surprise!

The group were all so intent on praying, they hadn't even heard the knock at the door. Harvey listened in on their prayers.

---

[175] Acts 12:10
[176] Acts 12:11
[177] Acts 12:12-13

One of them was currently saying, "Lord, nothing is too hard for you. The entire Roman army, which seems so insurmountable to all of us, is but a flea to you. You know that Peter—our brother, our friend, our leader, our teacher—has been captured. Please, Lord, do not let the Romans and the Jewish leaders succeed in their vile plots against us. Please allow Peter to be free—"

"He's here! He's outside!" The voice belonged to the servant girl whom Harvey had passed in the hallway. She was beaming with excitement and nearly yelling. "It's Peter! It's Peter!"[178]

"Rhoda! Be silent, young lady!" said the man who had been praying only seconds ago. "We are in the middle of very important prayers to God. Do not come in here and interrupt us!"

"But you are praying for *Peter*! And he's right outside!"

"You're out of your mind!"[179] said the man.

There was a knock at the door.

Harvey giggled to himself. "Oh," he said, "she didn't open the door. She left Peter outside. This is rich!"

The knock resulted in a moment of silence, but shortly the man who'd been praying spoke up again, "No, it can't be him. He's in prison!"

"I saw him with my own eyes!" said the girl identified as Rhoda. "He's right outside!"

"Oh, so he just *walked out*, is that it?" said the man sarcastically. "Just took a stroll out of his cell, where he's being guarded day and night, to come say hi to all of us?"

Harvey's laughter, unheard by all but himself, grew louder.

"I don't know," said the girl, "but he's here! I know what he looks like, I know what he sounds like, and he is standing outside the door right now!"

There was another knock at the door. The man again paused. Harvey's laughter was now peppered with a considerable amount of knee-slapping.

"It ... it must be his angel. It can't be him."

Harvey's laughter ceased. "What?" he said aloud. "His angel? Geez,

---

[178] Acts 12:14
[179] Acts 12:15

these are the leaders of the church! What are you talking about man, his *angel*? What does that even mean?"

The huddled group sat in silence, except for Rhoda who paced back and forth in frustration.

Yet another knock came at the door.

Rhoda stopped her pacing and spoke again. "You were literally just praying for his release! Do you not believe that God can do what you asked?"

She glared around at the room. Harvey smiled. "Oh, I like you," he said.

"Well fine," said the girl, after there was no response. "But *someone* is obviously at the door and I'm going to open it!"

She charged off towards the door, and immediately the group rose to their feet and followed her, crowding into the hallway to see what would happen.

Just as yet another knock came at the door, Rhoda opened it. Peter stood just outside, an expression of exasperation on his face (which gave Harvey another laugh).[180]

As soon as they saw him, everyone began talking excitedly at once. Peter motioned with his hand for them to be quiet.

They let him into the house, and shut the door. As he began telling them the story of how he had been rescued from prison, Harvey smiled to himself and decided that his work was done for tonight. He passed through the walls out of the house and into the night air.

Now it's time for Herod, thought Harvey.

~

It took Harvey some time to figure out exactly how to deal with Herod. He could have simply struck him down at any point, but this situation demanded justice that was a bit more of the poetic variety.

He found his way in via the people of Tyre and Sidon, who had been at odds with Herod and were increasingly suffering for it.

First, using Vox's power, Harvey stirred up fear among their

---

[180] Acts 12:16-17

leaders. If Herod should turn against them, would he go so far as to refuse to allow them to buy and sell from the other surrounding, subjugated nations? What if they couldn't buy food? What would they do then?

Once the people were sufficiently primed, and ready to make nice with Herod, all that remained was to grant them an audience and get them to puff up the man's already over-inflated ego. This step didn't prove difficult. Herod's personal servant, Blastus, was a man who loved bribes. All Harvey needed to do was get Blastus together with the leaders, and their greed and fear did the rest. With Blastus' support, they were quickly granted an audience with King Herod, who had now moved on from Jerusalem and was staying in Caesarea.[181]

This was all more planning than Harvey was used to doing, and things moved more slowly than he liked. Still, he found it interesting using Vox's power. It didn't *make* anyone do anything, but rather it persuaded them using what was already there inside of them. Fears were exaggerated, pride was fed, greed was met with tremendous temptation. It was like setting a trap for an animal, and it was amazing how many of the humans acted exactly like an animal, never even considering the danger that awaited them. There were those who would resist and fight the temptation, for whom Vox's power held little danger, but they were disturbingly few and far between.

The day finally arrived when all the pieces were in place. Harvey, invisible to all of the humans, stood beaming next to Herod, who was wearing his fancy royal clothing and sitting on his fancy throne, delivering his fancy speech to the people of Tyre and Sidon.[182] Herod used all of the usual, flowery language that the human political leaders had at their disposal when trying to gain the support of the masses. He told them all about their grand and glorious partnership with the Roman empire and how together they were all strong and blah blah blah. Some among the audience even seemed to be buying it. It was amazing how quickly even a conquered and subjugated people could convince themselves that their conquerors somehow had their good in mind.

---

[181] Acts 12:19-20
[182] Acts 12:21

As Herod's speech meandered along, Harvey was busy using Vox's power on those among the audience, especially the leaders: *Wasn't this speech amazing? Listen to the authority and majesty of this man Herod. Why, 'king' is not even a good enough title for him, is it? Perhaps some flowery words of response are in order. Maybe tell him how great he is. Perhaps you could get on his good side and secure a good position for you and your family. Yeah, that's right, think of the food, the money, the riches, the power ...*

As Herod's speech ended, one of the leaders of Tyre spoke up: "What a glorious speech! This is not the voice of a mere man, this is the voice of a *god*!" Many of the others shouted a hearty agreement.[183]

"Here we go," said Harvey, preparing to deliver the final blow.

"Thank you! Thank you all!" said Herod. "It is true, the divine nature of kings is such that—"

Herod slumped, suddenly dead.[184] The audience gasped in unison, and then silence poured over the area. Herod's body slid awkwardly down his throne and onto the floor with a sickening thud. His servant Blastus rushed onto the stage and moved close to his master.

He reached Herod but, upon seeing him, backed away in disgust. There was something happening to the body. Something was moving, *wriggling*.

"Wha ... are those ... worms?" said Blastus.

Harvey laughed to himself. "Oh man, Masheet was right about the worms. What a great touch!"

Herod's body was covered in thousands of them. They were already devouring him. The humans standing around were amazed and horrified.

Harvey planted a thought in the head of one of the leaders of Sidon. The man said aloud, "He's not a god. He's just a man like all of us. Gods don't get eaten by worms. An actual god must have been angry with him for saying that! That's why he died in this way!"

Harvey planted another thought, and another man said, "Didn't that man Peter, the one they say performs all those miracles and healings, who tells everyone to follow Jesus, escape miraculously from

---

[183] Acts 12:22
[184] Acts 12:23

Herod's clutches?"

"That oughta do it!" said Harvey with a smile.

As the people slowly recovered from their shock and began discussing what had happened and what to do next, Harvey flew up, eager to finally return to heaven and the presence of God.

And the word of God continued to spread and flourish.[185]

---

[185] Acts 12:24

Saul's Fall: How Four Men Changed the World

In Jerusalem, things were changing.

Since Jesus had died and risen again, the movement had been growing and what was once a small group of diehard followers had erupted to thousands.[186] The apostles—Peter in particular—were performing miracles as if they were Jesus himself.[187] The sick and injured from all around Jerusalem and the surrounding area were coming to be healed.

And other believers were arising too, men who were not apostles and were not with Jesus while he walked the earth. They were speaking boldly to their friends and some even engaged in public debate with religious leaders who were only used to squabbling betwixt their own factions.

Unfortunately, the young man Barnabas was not one of these bold men. He loved Jesus and he was determined to follow him even unto death, but boldness was never his strong suit. God had given him other gifts. He was filled with joy and was a constant encouragement to others in the church. Indeed, many of his friends didn't seem to remember that his given name wasn't *actually* Barnabas, which means Son of Encouragement.[188]

Still he longed to do more—longed to *be* more. He saw around him the hurting and the lost—those to whom darkness was so normal that they didn't even realize they were in it—and desperately wanted to be a light to them. But he was afraid. He didn't know how to approach them.

This longing led him to Stephen, whose own boldness would make a lion jealous. Barnabas had watched Stephen amaze people with miracles and wonders.[189] He gave his time to and talked with the very

---

[186] Acts 2:41, 2:47, 4:4, 5:14, 6:1
[187] Acts 3:1-8, 5:12-16, 5:18-20
[188] Acts 4:36
[189] Acts 6:5, 6:8

lowest beggars on the street corners and the very highest religious leaders in the temple as if they all held equal status. When Barnabas sheepishly approached Stephen and asked to spend some time with him ministering to the people of Jerusalem, he was accepted immediately.

So it was that Barnabas followed Stephen and preached both in temple and on street corner. At first the anxiety was almost overwhelming, but after a few trips he began to grow more comfortable in his role.

One day Stephen and Barnabas were witnessing about Jesus in the marketplace when a group of Jews approached them. At their head was a man who looked much too young to be leading this group.

"Excuse me, sirs, but we have seen you speaking about this man Jesus many a time, and we would like to talk to you as well," said their young leader.

Stephen and Barnabas turned to them. Barnabas smiled warmly, as was his custom when meeting anyone new.

"Hello," said Stephen. "And who are you?"

"We are from the Synagogue of the Freedmen,"[190] replied the young man. "Jews from outside of Judea and Galilee. My name is Saul. I know of you, Stephen, but who is this man?"

"I'm Barnabas."

"Fine, fine. Now, listen, as I say we've been watching you talk about this man Jesus, filling the air and people's hearts with your lies and wickedness."

Well, thought Barnabas, *he got right to the point. At least we know why they're here.*

Saul continued, "How can you continue on like this? You openly talk about this man Jesus as if he was the Messiah. He's dead! The Romans killed him! Everything that liar said while he lived amounted to nothing! You should stop peddling your lies and turning these people away from God!"

A small crowd began to gather around. Many of them had seen Stephen engaged in discussions exactly like this one, and they were

---

[190] Acts 6:9

hoping for a good show.

Stephen replied, "The Romans did indeed kill him, as you say, but it was at the request of you and people like you. Was there ever a prophet that your ancestors did not kill? But God has raised him from the dead, just as the scriptures foretold. If he hadn't died, maybe then an argument could be made that he wasn't from God, but the rejection of him by the enemies of God is further proof of who he is."

"The enemies of God!" cried Saul, his short fuse having already run its course. "You spread lies and deceit, and you call *us* enemies? You are the enemies!"

"We do not spread lies," said Stephen. "You have heard about all that Jesus is doing. By his power, even his apostles drive out evil spirits, and heal the sick, the blind, and the lame." He turned to the crowd, which was growing by the second as more and more people nearby took notice. "Who here doesn't know someone who has been healed by the power of Jesus?"

Many in the crowd suddenly grew quiet and very interested in their feet. Most of them were there to see a show, not to take part in one. Few wanted to get on the wrong side of the religious leaders.

"Hmph," said Saul, his anger temporarily subsiding. "You say a dead man lives, but where's the proof? You turn to these people for appeal, but no one says anything because they know you aren't from God."

"I ... I saw something." The voice belonged to a young girl, who had stepped forward before her mother could stop her. "I saw Jesus, when I was little. He came to our village, to Nain. He raised Seth back to life, and he had been dead for a whole day!"

Saul sneered. "The child doesn't know what she's sayi—"

"It's true," said the girl's mother. "I saw it with my own eyes. His poor mother was a widow and left with nothing. We were carrying him in the coffin to bury him when Jesus approached. When he saw Seth's mother, he said, 'Don't cry!' Then he told Seth to get up, and he did!"[191]

Saul started to respond but was instantly cut off by another

---

[191] Luke 7:11-15

bystander. "I saw Peter heal my sick brother. He was good as new!"[192]

"My friend just stood near Peter and let his shadow pass over her, and she was completely healed," said another woman in the crowd.[193]

Another spoke up, and then another, until almost everyone was excitedly talking at once about all the miraculous things they had seen and heard in the past few years. After a moment Stephen motioned for them to be quiet and turned back to Saul and his group.

"Jesus died, as you say," said Stephen. "But do you not know the scriptures or the power of God? Of course he suffered. Did Isaiah not say as much? Of course he was rejected. Of course he died. Did the scriptures not say all of these things? But now God has raised him back to life, and he cannot die again. He is the reigning king forever, just as the scriptures foretold. You are hard-hearted, just like your ancestors. Repent and turn to God, perhaps he will forgive all that you've done."

"Repent? Me? You wicked, filthy man! I follow the teachings of Moses and the prophets, given to us by God! I am a true child of Abraham!"

Seeing the conflict escalating before him, Barnabas finally spoke up, hoping to calm both Saul and Stephen. "My friend," he said to Saul in a warm tone, "we are Jews, just like you, and children of Abraham, too. God has blessed us as his chosen people. But being a physical descendant of Abraham is not enough. God's children are all those who do his will. Surely you see God at work in all of these healings? How could Peter's mere shadow heal sickness if not for the power of God at work in him?"

"Do not call me *friend*, you wicked snake! You and that deceiver Peter twist the words of Abraham and Moses to your own selfish ends! I, and these with me, are careful to follow the laws Moses passed down. We are true children of Abraham and God."

"Are you?" said Stephen. He turned to the crowd again. "Tell me, has this man Saul's shadow ever healed anyone, that you know of?" The crowd laughed. "Perhaps God likes Peter a little better, eh?" There was another round of laughter.

Saul's face turned even more crimson. "You mock me—us!—openly

---

[192] Acts 5:16
[193] Acts 5:15

Saul's Fall: How Four Men Changed the World

in public! Maybe you two will share the same fate as your precious Jesus!"

"I sure hope so," said Stephen as Saul and his group stormed off.

The crowd began to disperse, as it was now clear that the brief show was over.

"Perhaps you should not have antagonized him so much," said Barnabas.

"Don't be afraid, Barnabas," said Stephen. "Men like him can only kill the body, and after that they can do no more."

"I am not afraid ... okay, maybe I am afraid," said Barnabas. "But that's not what I mean. Jesus was filled with grace and truth. Perhaps in this case a little grace would go farther than a lot of truth."

"Maybe you're right, though honestly I can't see any way a man like that would ever truly turn to God," said Stephen. "He met us for about two minutes before he threatened to murder us."

Barnabas smiled one of his warm smiles. "Nothing is too hard for God, right? Perhaps he has plans even for a man like that."

Stephen shrugged and then turned back to the few who were still watching them expectantly and continued his preaching.

~

While things were changing in Jerusalem, far away in Damascus things were staying very much the same.

This was a city very different from Jerusalem. It was far to the northeast, well outside of Israel. A trading hub, Damascus was wealthy, multi-cultural, and dangerous to any who weren't careful to keep an eye on their belongings. Among the other residents, the city supported a large Jewish community and multiple synagogues.

Ananias was one of the many Jews who called this place home. Out here, the stories about Jesus were just that: stories. They were interesting tales of a man who had apparently caused quite a stir in Galilee and Judea—and even more so in Jerusalem itself—before his death. Even now there were rumors of healings and large groups of followers growing in Jerusalem. But here in Damascus, day-to-day life was the same as Ananias had ever remembered it being.

He spent his days like many other Jews in the city. He was a tent-maker by trade, and the steady flow of travelers through Damascus ensured there was plenty of trade to be had. He closely followed the Jewish laws and traditions, an act that earned him the respect of those around him. Even the Gentiles that he knew, who didn't understand the Jewish law, seemed to have a kind of respect for him and his ways.

In short, Ananias was perfectly respectable but otherwise not particularly noteworthy. He was not the kind of man that anyone would assume was destined for great things or would play some kind of crucial role in human history. After all, such things are done by kings with shining swords or important prophets who perform miracles or wandering preachers who risk their lives daily and never know where their next meal is coming from. Men who make tents every day, perform simple kindnesses for their neighbors, and make sure to take one day off a week because God said to rarely factor into things.

The average person would not think too highly of Ananias. But God is not the average person.

~

There was a moment before the first stone struck where Barnabas was still in disbelief, where it seemed that maybe, just maybe, some last-minute intercession would rescue Stephen from the swift death that awaited him. In that moment, the events of the past few days kept replaying themselves in his head.

It had all happened so quickly. Saul was ruthless and much more clever than he had appeared at first when he argued with them in the marketplace. He was back the next day with a fresh set of arguments and a larger group of followers. Stephen again refuted him and again won over the crowd, and Saul left that day humiliated just as the day before.[194] But then he was back again the next day, and the next day, and the next.

---

[194] Acts 6:10

At first Barnabas had wondered how such a young man had gained such a following as this, but he understood it now. Saul was the most tenacious man Barnabas had ever met. He attacked everything with his misguided zeal and there was no deterring him once he made up his mind. He would stoop to any level to accomplish his goal. Most likely men were too afraid *not* to follow him.

Eventually Saul had grown tired of losing arguments and resorted to a different approach. He began spreading rumors among the people and even talking directly to the Sanhedrin, saying that Stephen spoke blasphemy against God and Moses.[195] Barnabas could only watch as Stephen was brought before the Sanhedrin, found guilty by what was now more an enraged mob than a group of respectable religious leaders, and then dragged outside the city.[196] And now ...

And now they threw the first stone.

It landed with an audible thud followed by a grunt from Stephen. That first stone seemed to break the spell that held back the others, and shortly the entire surrounding group of men were throwing vicious stones with all their might at Stephen. Barnabas' mentor was being murdered right before his eyes.

With Stephen's strength and consciousness rapidly leaving him, he cried out, "Lord Jesus, receive my spirit!"[197] He fell to his knees. Stone after stone wracked his body and blood was already gushing from the wounds on his head. With his final words, Stephen cried out again, "Lord, do not hold this sin against them!"[198]

And then he fell, dead. The dark deed was done, but more stones were thrown just for good measure. The sound of the rocks striking the recent corpse turned Barnabas' stomach.

He turned to where Saul was standing, off to the side, with the cloaks of the various religious leaders at his feet so that they wouldn't get any of Stephen's blood on them.[199]

Barnabas was surprised to see that Saul was already looking back at

---

[195] Acts 6:12-14
[196] Acts 7:57-58
[197] Acts 7:59
[198] Acts 7:60
[199] Acts 7:58

him. He had seemed to be waiting for an opportunity to catch his eye, while no one else was watching. Now that he had that opportunity, he silently mouthed the words to Barnabas, "You're next."

Barnabas ran. He didn't even stop for supplies. Fear carried him, and his pace did not slow until he could no longer see Jerusalem behind him.

~

Ananias neatly put his tools away. The day's work was done and Ananias was in high spirits. It had been a productive day; he'd completed six tents, just shy of his record of seven. His young son worked by his side, and while his help only barely offset the time Ananias had to take explaining and admonishing, Ananias loved having him there. It made the day pass so much more quickly.

But now it was time to eat, drink, and relax with his family. He thought to himself that Solomon had it right when he said that it is good for people to eat, drink, and enjoy their work.[200] Ananias had experienced the same troubles as any other man, and had had his share of sadness, misery, and long nights spent awake and wondering what it was all for. But somehow as long as his hands were busy with his tents and he had loved ones around him, it all seemed less burdensome.

He gathered up his day's product and made his way to the marketplace, his young son in tow with a small bundle of his own. He had a deal with one of the traders there who would give him a good price. Ananias could cut out the middle man and make a little more money if he made the tents while manning a small store of his own, but he never much liked haggling and then he couldn't do his work out of his home with his family.

He sold the tents and began heading back home when his son stopped him.

"Dad?"

"Yes?"

---

[200] Ecclesiastes 5:18

"What's that man doing?" The boy pointed a finger at a young man sitting by the side of the road. This was, unfortunately, not a rare sight in a large city like Damascus. The poor and homeless were everywhere, begging or stealing or making a living in any other way they could think of.

"He's not doing anything," said Ananias.

"He looks like a beggar, dad."

"Yes, he probably is."

"But he doesn't look right," said the boy.

Ananias stared a moment longer at the young man, and had to admit to himself that his son was right. Something about the man looked off. Ananias walked by beggars every day. They came in many shapes and sizes but one thing they all had in common: even after only a few weeks or months they grew accustomed to and even comfortable in their role. This man looked anything but comfortable. He looked scared and confused. This was not a man familiar with begging on a street corner.

Ananias walked towards the man. "Be careful," he said to his son, "and stay behind me so that I am between you and him, just in case."

As he drew closer, he noticed another detail about the young man, something that had obviously been nagging his subconscious and was now finally bubbling up to his conscious thoughts: the man appeared to be Jewish.

Ananias sat down to his left, and his son sat obediently on the other side of his father.

"Hello, friend," said Ananias.

"Hello," said the young man, with a mixture of hope and suspicion in his voice.

"Are you new to Damascus?"

"Yes. I came here from Jerusalem."

"Ah," said Ananias, "I thought so. You are Jewish, just like me. I'm Ananias."

"I'm Barnabas—er, Joseph."

Ananias smiled. "A man with two names? Barnabas, 'son of encouragement', that's quite a name. I'd love to hear how you earned that. But first, you look out of place here. What brings you to

Damascus?"

The young man began to relax a little. For a brief moment he seemed to be dealing with some inner struggle, but then he made a decision. "In truth," he said, "I'm running away from a man who wants to kill me. Damascus was the farthest away place I could think of."

Ananias unsuccessfully stifled a laugh. Barnabas gave him a questioning look.

"I'm sorry," said Ananias with a smile, "I'm not trying to make light of your situation. It's just something my dad used to say about people from Jerusalem. He said they thought the whole world revolved around that city. So when you said that Damascus was the farthest away place you could think of … well let's just say there are much farther places. The world is quite a bit bigger than the maps in Jerusalem tend to show."

Ananias was worried he may have offended the young man, but instead Barnabas only smiled and laughed himself. "Perhaps I have been there too long," said Barnabas between chuckles.

"Do you have somewhere to stay?" asked Ananias.

"No," admitted Barnabas. "Nor do I have food. I ran so quickly I did not even pack anything. I made it here from Jerusalem on anything I could gather on the way and with what little money I had on my person, which is now gone."

"Perhaps I can help you," said Ananias, "but please understand that first I must know what it is you did that provoked someone to kill you. You don't seem like that kind of person. Even when you are low like this, you speak kindly and are even able to laugh at yourself."

Barnabas did not hesitate before he responded. "I am in danger because I belong to Jesus, whom the religious leaders killed but God raised to life. A man named Saul is growing in power among the Jews in Jerusalem and he is determined to imprison or kill all who believe in Jesus. He murdered my mentor, Stephen, right before my very eyes."

"Ah," said Ananias, "so you are a member of 'The Way', as I've heard it referred to. I've never met any of you before, but interesting rumors of miracles have reached my ears even here at 'the farthest away place' you can think of."

"They are not rumors," said Barnabas. "Just as I saw Stephen murdered with these very eyes, so have I seen men healed of all kinds of affliction; the blind made to see, the lame made to walk, and even dead men brought back to life. Jesus did these things while he was still with us, and now his apostles do them. The miracles are God's proof of who Jesus is. God promised long ago a messiah and king for his people the Jews, and Jesus is exactly that, only not in the way many were expecting. Any who believe in him will have their sins forgiven and be saved. This includes you, Ananias."

Ananias was quiet for a moment before he responded again. "I think I see now why you may be in this trouble. I don't think I've ever met a man so bold."

"Bold?" said Barnabas, surprised.

"Yes, I've known you all of two minutes and already you are telling me I should be completely changing my life." Ananias stood up and his son followed suit. "Why don't you come and stay with me for a while? Do you know anything about making tents?"

"Not a thing," said Barnabas, as he also stood up.

"Well, how about I teach you about tents, and you tell me more about this Jesus fellow and all that's happened to you?"

Barnabas smiled. The two men and the boy headed off towards Ananias' home.

~

In Jerusalem, a small group of believers huddled together in a tiny house, waiting for the inevitable. They did not have to wait long.

A gruff knock came at the door. One of those in the house peered out and confirmed their fears.

"It's him," he whispered. "It's Saul."

There was another knock on the door.

"Open it, now, or these Roman soldiers with me will break it down!"

"What do we do?" whispered one of the men.

"I don't—"

The flimsy wooden door burst open, the lock not even holding up to a single strike from the soldier. Saul strode in through the dust and stood in the center of the room. He looked around at the huddled and terrified group.

"Do you follow Jesus?" he asked plainly.

"Yes," said one without hesitation despite his obvious fear. He stood up. The others followed suit.

"Excellent," said Saul. "You know, almost everywhere I've gone they admit it almost instantly, just like you. It really makes things easier." Saul unraveled a scroll. "What I have here are official papers from the Roman government authorizing the arrest and imprisonment of all of you and anyone else who incites rebellion and unrest by proclaiming the teachings of Jesus."

He turned to the soldiers behind him. "Take them."

The soldiers rushed in and pulled everyone out the house.[201] The last man tried to resist, but a few blows from a couple of the soldiers quickly put an end to his struggle.

As he was being dragged out, Saul said, "Wait." The soldiers immediately stopped. Saul took a step forward and bent down so that he was face-to-face with the man.

"Tell me, do you know where I can find Barnabas?" asked Saul.

The man did not reply.

"If you tell me, I promise to let you go. In fact, all of those who were here with you, they will all go free if you tell me where Barnabas is."

"I don't know," said the man.

"That's what everyone has told me so far," said Saul. "I'm beginning to think you are lying to me. You would sin against God by bearing false witness against Barnabas?"

"It's true, I don't know," said the man. "Nobody knows. He just disappeared around the time you kil—I mean around the time Stephen was killed. I don't know where he is."

"Just disappeared," said Saul sarcastically. "What a shame that you couldn't save yourself and your friends. Well I guess it's off to the prison with you."

The man was dragged out of the house.

---

[201] Acts 8:1-3

Several months passed. Barnabas would later remember those months fondly as one of the best and most refreshing times in his life. Before he met Ananias, he thought he might die, either from being caught by Saul, being attacked on the road, or from starvation. But now he was living with Ananias, surrounded by his loving family, and with plenty to eat and plenty to do.

He spent his days learning tent-making from Ananias. It took some time, but he was starting to get good at it and could make one worthy of selling. He was happy to finally be able to pay Ananias back for at least some of the good he'd done for him.

In the evenings, Barnabas tried at first to relax with Ananias and his family and keep to himself, making every attempt to remain anonymous. But all around him in the city he saw the hurting and the lost. Indeed, he couldn't *not* see it. He saw those who were crushed under the weight of slavery or oppression. He saw others who were slaves to alcohol, or sexual sins, or any number of the other vices that destroy men and bring them a slow death without even realizing it. It was as if Jesus had opened his eyes, and they couldn't be closed again. He couldn't un-see these things, and having seen them he couldn't remain quiet about the savior who could rescue from them all.

So he began going out in the evenings to the marketplaces, just as he would with Stephen so many months ago, and spoke to both Jews and Gentiles. And on the Sabbath he visited the synagogues and tried to reason with the Jews there. Ananias had called him "bold" when he first met him, and he couldn't believe that anyone could think that about him. But perhaps that was truly what he had become.

The tent-making continued, but more and more Barnabas considered it to be his secondary job; just a way to make enough money to continue doing the *real* work that God had called him to. He often thought to himself that if he ever came across others in his situation—called to preach Jesus' message in a foreign city—he should teach them how to make tents. It was an ideal way to make a living while still having time to teach and preach.

Ananias was the first to believe. He listened patiently as Barnabas spoke to him, and he spent time examining the scriptures to see if what Barnabas said was true. Barnabas was amazed that an older man would humbly listen to and accept the truth of what Barnabas was saying, despite the fact that Barnabas was young and essentially a beggar when Ananias met him.

There were others who quickly accepted the message as well. Soon there was a small church meeting in Ananias' house. Barnabas taught them everything he knew about Jesus' message. It all happened so quickly that Barnabas knew it must be the work of God. These hearts had been softened to his message long before he arrived.

There was another thing happening, which Barnabas wasn't sure what to do with. It wasn't only the Jews who were turning to Jesus, but Gentiles in the city were doing it as well. Barnabas often thought about what some of the leaders of the church back in Jerusalem would have said if they knew he'd begun accepting Gentiles among the believers. Surely at least some would resist it. But Barnabas had made up his mind; if God was going to show his approval by giving faith and the Holy Spirit to these Gentiles, then who was he to go against that? Even if someone like Peter were to chastise him, should he choose to listen to Peter rather than God?

All the while stories and rumors of the persecution happening in Jerusalem found their way even to Damascus. The young man Saul had grown in power almost overnight. Many were being arrested and others were fleeing. A few of those even made their way to Damascus, where Barnabas found homes for them and helped them get on their feet.

Barnabas was so happy he'd come to Damascus. It was beginning to feel like a peaceful refuge where believers could really flourish. The church was growing almost every week, and while there was some opposition among the other Jews in the city, the people here were generally safe and free to follow Jesus without fear. He thought, perhaps, he'd found a new home.

~

"Damascus?" asked Caiaphas, the high priest.[202] "Are you quite certain?"

"I am," said Saul. He smiled at the high priest and the other assembled members of the Sanhedrin. "Apparently quite a large number of them, and growing every day."

"It's hard to believe," said one of the elders. "How could this blasphemy have spread so far away in such a short time?"

"I ask only for the permission to find out," replied Saul. "Please give me your official approval and some men to take with me, and I will go investigate the matter myself and bring back any followers of The Way I find in Damascus. I will imprison them just as I have imprisoned those here in Jerusalem."[203]

A grey-haired man, a Pharisee and elder, stood up, and immediately all eyes fixed on him.

"Gamaliel," said Saul with a deceptive smile, "my mentor, master, and friend. Please speak your mind."[204]

Gamaliel responded, "Could this not having something to do with this Barnabas fellow you've been after? I've heard some of these reports you speak of about The Way in Damascus, and apparently that young man is at the head of it all."

Saul's smile faltered, but was quickly reapplied. "I was right to be after him. You see how dangerous he is. His false tongue is teaching lies and blaspheming God, and convincing others to do the same."

"Caiaphas," said Gamaliel, turning to the high priest, "I do not think we should do this. This feels more like a personal vendetta than the work of God. Saul is young yet. Perhaps this responsibility should go to somebody with a cooler head."

Saul's smile again evaporated, and this time it did not return. Gamaliel was well-respected and had personally been Saul's teacher, as everyone present was well aware. His opinion of Saul carried tremendous weight.

Gamaliel continued, "I'm not even sure we should be doing anything at all. If this is not from God, it will soon fail. If it is from God,

---

[202] Matthew 26:3, Matthew 26:57, John 11:49, John 18:13, John 18:24, Acts 4:6
[203] Acts 9:2
[204] Acts 5:34, Acts 22:3

nothing we do can stop it."

"Isn't that what he said before?"[205] said Saul, barely containing his rage "That we should do nothing? Doing nothing accomplished just that—nothing! But in this short time where we've taken *action*, The Way has been almost snuffed out! Please, Caiaphas, allow me to finish the job."

"Snuffed out?" responded Gamaliel. "From your description, it sounds more like it's spreading, even reaching farther than Galilee! Didn't I say that if it's from God we cannot stop it? All of your actions, Saul, have served only to spread it further."[206]

The high priest finally interjected himself. "What is it you are saying, Gamaliel? You are implying that men like Peter and Barnabas are from God. You are a wise man and an expert in the law and the prophets, so surely you understand that this is not true. Sit down, please."

A humiliating silence washed over the whole Sanhedrin. Seconds passed but each felt more like a minute. Gamaliel, his face flushed, said nothing further and sat down.

"Saul," said the high priest, "you may have the official approval you seek. We will draw up the papers and you can leave as soon as you'd like."

Saul smiled. "I leave tomorrow morning at sunrise."

~

The assembled church members outside of Ananias' home all listened expectantly to Barnabas. There were so many of them now that they typically would meet in different homes separately, with a few of those who had fled from Jerusalem appointed by Barnabas to lead the various groups. But now they all met together. Most of them already had a pretty good idea of what Barnabas was about to say, but nevertheless they wanted to hear it to confirm.

Barnabas began, "He's coming. Saul is coming *here*. He will arrive in

---

[205] Acts 5:34-39
[206] Acts 8:4

a few days at the most, and more likely in a day or two."

Jesse, a man known for a somewhat quick temper, immediately spoke up. "You said we'd be safe here! You'd said they'd never come here!"

"I thought they wouldn't," said Barnabas. "We're not even in Galilee, much less Judea. I didn't think they'd ever care what happened up here."

"We're going to die!" Jesse shouted.

"Is Jesus worth dying for?" asked another man, turning to Jesse.

Slowly, Jesse's anger softened. "Yes," he relented, "I just really don't want to."

Barnabas couldn't help but smile. Jesse's quick temper had led to a string of broken relationships in his life and left him friendless and desperate. Not too long ago, he would surely have stormed out at this kind of news and broken off all contact with the rest of the church. He had turned to Jesus only recently, but Barnabas could already see the changes happening in him.

He looked around at the rest of the church. "Listen," he said. "Jesus is worth dying for, but we don't know what's going to happen. We know exactly what to do right now. We pray. We meet together and pray every day until he gets to Damascus, and every day after he arrives. All he can do is kill our bodies. Our souls are safe and our lives are eternal so long as we keep our hope in Jesus."

So, the church prayed.

~

Saul—riding his donkey and surrounded by the other men sent by the Jewish leaders—crested the hill and caught his first good sight of Damascus. It wouldn't be long now. His journey of multiple days was nearing an end and soon his real work could begin.

He'd had a lot of time on the journey to think about what to do once he got to Damascus. First, he'd head to the local synagogues to ask questions and find out as much as he could. There may be sympathizers among them, but surely there would be those *true* God-fearing men who would speak honestly and tell him where to find the members of The Way.

And once he found Barnabas, the man who helped Stephen humiliate him all those times ...

The words of Gamaliel flashed through Saul's mind once again: "This feels more like a personal vendetta than the work of God." That confrontation with his former teacher had tormented him for days. His anger welled up within him again, and he began talking to the man next to him.

"Do you know that when I got permission to come to Damascus, my own teacher and mentor Gamaliel opposed me?"

The man, who'd heard and reheard this story many times already, nodded.

"I do not understand why he is so blind to this. These members of The Way are a group of foolish and evil men, bent on destroying Israel's laws and traditions. Isn't it enough that we have to fight for our way of life under the thumb of the Romans? And now we have wicked people like this who want to destroy us from within. A man as wise and learned as Gamaliel should understand that in order to be holy as God has demanded we must root out this evil from among us."

The man nodded again. The many days spent on this journey had taught him that when Saul began ranting like this, a simple nod was best.

"Do you think God will ever rescue us from the Romans if we continue allowing this kind of disobedience? And all of it in the name of this man Jesus. No one can deny that he did amazing things, and even I myself can't explain them except to say that he must have been some kind of evil magician, but he died and came to nothing. Is that our king? Where is his throne? Where are his people? Where is his army? He did not overthrow the Romans. He did not liberate our people. He has not restored Israel to the glorious times of David and Solomon, when all the world knew our power and the blessings bestowed upon us as God's children. The Romans killed him, and that was the end of—"

A sudden, blinding light flashed from the sky, and more than a light. It had substance to it; a force; a kind of light that somehow had density. Saul instinctively closed his eyes and was unable to prevent himself from falling to the ground off of the donkey. The wind was knocked out of him and for a brief moment he thought he might die. But slowly he found himself able to breathe again. He didn't dare open his eyes again, too terrified that he would go blind if he looked for even a second.

And then a voice—a deep, terrifying voice that felt like it was coming from everywhere and nowhere, from both outside himself and inside his own head—boomed, "Saul, Saul, why do you persecute me?"

Saul thought about Jesus, whom he was talking about only seconds ago. But no, it couldn't be. "Who are you, Lord?" he asked.

"I *am* Jesus, whom you are persecuting," said the voice. "Now, get up! Go into the city! You will be told what you must do."

And then it was quiet. No one made a sound.

Saul wanted to open his eyes, but they still burned from the light. It wasn't until he got to his feet that he risked opening them again. When he did so, it was as if he hadn't. The light had completely blinded him.

"Are you still there?" he asked.

"We are all still here," came the reply of the man he'd been speaking to. "What was that voice? Where did it come from? Why did you fall?"

"The light it ... it knocked me to the ground. The light blinded me. I can't see anything."

"What light?"

"You didn't see it? How could you not see it?" Saul reached out his hands, unsure of even which direction he was facing. "Please, help me. I can't see."

The man reached out his hand so Saul could grasp it.

"What should we do now?" said the man.

"The voice—Jesus, it was Jesus—said to go into the city. Let's go into Damascus and find a place to stay and wait. I will pray and wait."

The man tugged at Saul to indicate the direction of Damascus. The party of men continued on in silence until they reached the city and found a place to stay among the local Jews.[207]

---

[207] Acts 9:3-8, Acts 22:6-11

~

"Any news on Saul yet?" asked Ananias.

"No," said Barnabas. "What they are saying is that he hasn't left the house even once since he arrived three days ago. I even heard that he's been refusing to eat or drink."[208]

"Nothing to drink for three days?" said Ananias. "I don't know what to make of that. How are the others in the church taking it?"

"Some of them are happy and praising God that we have been rescued from this man. Others are saying it's some kind of trick, that he's spreading rumors about Jesus talking to him so that he can get in good with the believers and find out where we all live. Others don't know what to think, and they're just waiting to see what happens."

Ananias smiled. "Well, if he hasn't come looking for us yet after three days, I think it's safe to say we've been rescued. It's hard to believe, isn't it? Only a few days ago we were terrified for our lives. I thought I might die or be imprisoned; I had no idea what would happen to my wife and kids. But God took care of it so easily, like it was nothing at all. Just a light and a few sentences, and it's all over, just like that. He makes it look so easy."

Barnabas laughed. "Yes, it shouldn't surprise us but I'll admit I'm blown away as well."

They worked in silence for a while longer before Ananias spoke up again. "He really hasn't had anything to drink in three days?"

"As far as I know, yes."

"That's hard to believe. If it were anyone else, I'd think he was humbling himself, but you've described this man as anything but humble. He's an elite Jewish Pharisee and he knows it."

"Perhaps even he will turn to Jesus," said Barnabas.

"Would Jesus even save someone like that? A murderer who harms and destroys his people?"

The two again worked in silence for a few minutes. After a while, Ananias sent his son off to take a break and decided to give himself a short one as well. After drinking a bit of wine and relaxing for a short

---

[208] Acts 9:9

while, he went to a separate room to pray.

Immediately after closing his eyes, he saw a light in front of him, a light he could almost feel.

A voice came from the light. "Ananias!"[209]

"Yes, Lord?" answered Ananias. He had never before seen or heard anything like this, but he knew immediately who it must be.

"Go to the house of Judas, on Straight Street. Ask for a man from Tarsus named Saul. He is praying and in a vision he has seen a man named Ananias come and place his hands on him and restore his sight."

Ananias almost couldn't believe what he was hearing. Wasn't losing his sight the only thing that was keeping the church safe? "Lord," he said, "I have heard many reports about this man and all the harm he has done to your people in Jerusalem, and now he's come here to do the same thing to us. He wants to arrest everyone who calls on the name of Jesus, on your name."

"Go!" said the voice, and the tone of command was unmistakable. But then it softened. "This man is my chosen instrument to proclaim my name to the Gentiles and their kings and the people of Israel. I will show him how much he must suffer for my name."

Ananias almost opened his mouth to speak again, but then he remembered Moses' initial conversation with God and thought better of it.[210] "Yes, Lord," was all he said.

He opened his eyes to a very normal-looking room. The vision was gone.

He stood up and walked back to Barnabas.

"I have to go," he said.

"Go where?" asked Barnabas.

"I have to go to ... Straight Street. I have to go see Saul. Jesus told me to go and restore his sight. He is to become our brother, and even more as God has great plans for him."

Barnabas only stared at him for a few seconds. Ananias briefly wondered if the young man was going to call him crazy for saying something like that, or possibly even get angry. But after the silence, he

---

[209] Acts 9:10-16
[210] Exodus 4:14

stood up and said, simply, "Okay, then let's go."

The two made their way through the city on the short journey until they were finally at the house. As they approached the house, Ananias said, "Listen, I think I'm supposed to go in there alone. Jesus told me that Saul had seen a vision of me coming in and restoring his sight."

"Okay," said Barnabas, "I will wait out here."

Ananias knocked on the door, and shortly the owner of the house, Judas, answered. Upon seeing Ananias, Judas didn't even greet him, but said simply, "He's in here. Follow me."

Ananias was led to an inner room where he finally laid eyes on Saul for the first time. The man looked weak from his lack of food and water. He was sitting on the floor with his back against a wall, eyes starring forward into nothingness.

"You have to do something," said Judas. "He refuses all food and water. He won't live much longer if he goes on like this."

"It's okay," said Ananias. "He is not going to die."

Judas seemed to take Ananias at his word. He nodded and left the room.

Ananias stepped over to Saul and crouched down.[211] He placed his hands on him and said, "*Brother* Saul, the Lord Jesus who appeared to you on the road here has sent me to you so that you may see again and be filled with the Holy Spirit."

As Ananias watched, something fell from Saul's eyes. It looked like some kind of scale or skin. Immediately, Saul could see again and his eyes brightened. He looked into Ananias' face and smiled.

"The God of our ancestors chose you to know his will, see the Righteous One, and even hear the words from his mouth," said Ananias. "Now you will be his witness to all people of what you have seen and heard. Now, come with me. You must be baptized, just as Jesus commanded."

Ananias placed his arm around Saul and helped him to his feet. The man was weak but could still manage to walk with only a little support. When they left the house, Barnabas was waiting.

"Barnabas," said Saul, simply, but the word was filled with so much

---

[211] Acts 9:17-19, Acts 22:12-16

Saul's Fall: How Four Men Changed the World 129

sorrow and hope and pleading that Barnabas immediately ran to his side and placed his arm around him as well.

"It's okay," said Barnabas.

"Let's go down to the river," said Ananias, "he must be baptized. It's not far."

Together, the three headed to the bank. Ananias brought Saul out into the river, lowered him into the water until he was fully immersed, and then raised him back up again. He'd heard stories about momentous occasions such as this that happened up in Jerusalem and how they were accompanied by tongues of fire or earthquakes or powerful winds or people speaking in languages they didn't know. He was somewhat disappointed to see that absolutely nothing of the sort happened here. Even just a *little* earthquake would have been nice.

After the baptism, they brought Saul back to Ananias' house and gave him some food and drink, which he gladly took, and his strength began to return to him.

~

This is only the beginning of Saul's story, who was later known as Paul. In his lifetime he accomplished great things, preaching to Gentile groups that had previously never known Jesus, performing astounding miracles, and even bringing a boy back to life. He wrote more of the New Testament than any other author. He suffered greatly for the name of Jesus and was insulted, imprisoned, beaten, and even left for dead multiple times. But by that same name of Jesus he now lives again, forever, in all the joy and fulfillment of heaven, just as Jesus offers to all who call on his name.

Twelve Coats

The couple waited anxiously outside the entrance of the Tabernacle.[212] The curtain wall bowed and swayed with the wind. Beyond the curtain, they could only see the top of the structure surrounding the Holy Place inside. The man paced back and forth slightly.

"I'm still not so sure about this," said the man.

"It's fine. Besides, where else do we have to go?" said the woman. "This is the Tabernacle."

"Yes," said the man, "it may be the Tabernacle, but it's empty. The ark is gone. It's an empty shell now. And this boy is not Eli."

"Maybe so," said the woman, "but everyone says God talks to him. He can help us."

"He's a child. We are putting our hopes for a family in the words of a child."

"He's a man, even if only barely. But we are not putting our hopes in him; we are putting our hopes in God. He's God of everything, right? He can do anything, even without an ark and with a boy for a priest."

"Maybe so, but I'm still not sure about this," said the man once more.

Just then, Samuel arrived. Zits and patches of facial hair—the oft-embarrassing marks of the early teenager—riddled his face. Even the beautiful, multi-colored ephod he wore somehow looked awkward on the lanky young man. His long hair, which had never been cut from birth, was braided inexpertly, with stray hairs venturing out in all directions.

The man shot a look at his wife full of meaning, and she returned one full of a different meaning. As with any couple that had been together a long time, a few quick glances and small eye motions could contain paragraphs worth of dialogue or, in this case, argument.

Nevertheless, the couple stood to attention to hear what Samuel had to say.

The young man was before them for a short while before he spoke.

---

[212] Exodus 36-38

He seemed to be dreading whatever he was about to tell them. Finally, he said, "Yahweh says he will grant your request. Even now, your sick child has been healed, and when you return home you will find him sitting up and happy, with his grandmother rejoicing at his recovery. And Yahweh will grant you more children, too."

The couple stared, hardly believing what they were hearing. The young man had seemed so apprehensive about saying it, but everything he'd prophesied was positive, and neither was quite sure what to make of that.

The woman was the first to react. "Well ... that is fantastic news! Honey, did you hear that? That God should care about one little family like ours among all those in Israel who are suffering!"

"They do not seek God," said the young Samuel, "but you do. If everyone turned to God as you, and obeyed him, you can be sure he would not stop pouring out blessings on all Israel."

Despite the happy news, Samuel still shifted his feet uneasily.

"There's something more?" asked the man.

"Yes," said Samuel, with a slight crack in his voice that everyone present tried not to notice. "He also says to ... he says you must treat your workers fairly and stop withholding their wages. You beat them when they've done nothing wrong. You charge them for costs that you should bear the burden of. You treat them like slaves, though they are your Israelite brothers. Even your animals, too, you often do not allow them to rest on Sabbaths."

"I don't, I mean, I haven't, well, I mean, how did you kn—er, I mean, okay. That's not so bad." The man turned to his wife and tried to smile. "Right, sweetie? That's not so bad. We can do that. Right?"

"And ..." said Samuel, "he says he has seen the way you oppress them. If you turn from your ways and follow him with all of your heart and love your neighbor as yourself, he will bless you just as I have promised. But if you do not, he will blot you and your family out from the face of the earth and put someone else in your place. Every blessing you are given will be turned sour, and the curse will be even greater. Instead of healing grave illnesses, he will exacerbate small ones. Instead of bringing your children back from the brink of death, you'll lose them unexpectedly. But your workers will have justice and even your animals will be cared for properly by someone else."

Silence fell over all three of them. Try as he might to control it, the man's face turned a crimson color, and his wife began tearing up.

"I'm sorry but ... but that's what he said," said Samuel.

As the implications of this were still settling into the minds of the man and the woman, one of the young women who served outside of the Tabernacle approached.

"Samuel!" said the servant. "Hannah has arrived, with her whole family!"

Samuel's face immediately brightened. "Mommy?" he said, excitedly, before bolting off in the direction from which the servant had come.

The man turned to his wife, who also looked back at him. "*Mommy?*" he said with a roll of his eyes.

"Come on," responded his wife. "Let's go home and see our son. We have ... a lot to think about on the way."

Samuel ran to his mother and family. He threw his arms around his mother and buried his head in her shoulder to hide the tears that were even now starting. Behind her stood the rest of the large family: his five younger siblings, three brothers and two sisters, and his father Elkanah, along with his father's other wife Peninnah and her adult children.[213] It had been a year since he had last seen them all; they only came up to Shiloh once a year to sacrifice to Yahweh.[214]

He held his mother for what felt like several minutes. Then, finally, he released her and turned to the rest of his family. He warmly greeted his younger siblings, but didn't go much farther than simply acknowledging his father and his father's other wife and family. Samuel had always had mixed feelings about his father. Eli, the priest who raised him, was the only real father he ever knew, and somehow it felt like betrayal to show affection to this man he barely knew, even more so now that Eli was dead.

When the greetings were complete, Hannah turned to Elkanah and said, "Please, allow us a few minutes to catch up before the sacrifice."

He nodded.

---

[213] 1 Samuel 1:1-2, 1 Samuel 2:21
[214] 1 Samuel 1:3

After Hannah and Samuel had taken a couple of steps, she stopped and said, "Oh! I almost forgot!" She turned back and opened one of the sacks they brought on the trip. "Your coat!"

From the sack she pulled an expertly woven red wool coat with small details done in black. "I just finished this one last week," said Hannah. "I was afraid I wouldn't be done in time this year!"

The two headed off away from the rest of the family again. Hannah kept the coat tucked away and did not give it to Samuel just yet.

"Should we talk in Eli's house, mom?" asked Samuel.

"Don't you mean your house?" said Hannah. "It's yours now. Both he and his sons are dead, and you are now the priest at Shiloh. I'm sure he would have wanted you to have it."

Samuel didn't say anything in reply. The rest of the short journey was made in silence.

Once inside the house, Hannah pulled out the coat again so Samuel could examine it. He smiled and took it from her.

"It looks amazing!" he said.

"Good! I'm always worried that you won't like it. I wanted to wait until we got out of sight of the family to give it to you. You know how your brothers and sisters can be."

"No, I don't know how they can be," said Samuel, and he meant it. "I only see them once a year, and they never want to talk much. I'm a complete stranger to them."

"Well, they can be jealous, you know. Their famous brother, blessed by God, priest and prophet, gets a special coat, that sort of thing."

"Jealous?" said Samuel, shocked. "Jealous of what? Of me?"

"Well, yes," said his mother. "I know these coats are extravagant, but it's all I get to do for you all year. They don't understand that."

"Don't understand?" said Samuel, tremendous emotion suddenly filling his voice until he was almost yelling. "Don't understand? They have a family! They have a *mom*! All I get is a lousy coat!" Samuel threw the vibrant new coat onto the ground, but immediately regretted it. He carefully picked it up before sitting down with his back to the wall.

"I'm sorry," he said, failing to hold back the tears. "I'm sorry. I shouldn't have done that."

His mother, shocked at first by the sudden outburst, recovered and sat down next to him. She put her arm around his shoulder, but he remained motionless with his head buried in his hands.

"I'm sorry, mom," he said again. "I'm sorry."

"It's okay, my son, it's *okay*."

"It's not okay. Nothing is okay."

She held him quietly for a couple of minutes as the tears drained out, offering a cloth handkerchief when he needed it, and brushing away the wild strands of his hair when they ventured toward her face. The sobs eventually slowed and, finally, ceased altogether.

"I'm sorry, mom," he said yet again. "I don't know what's wrong."

"How long has it been now, since Eli died?" asked Hannah.

"Two months."

"And you've been the priest here all that time?"

"Yes."

"And the ark is gone?"

"Yes."

"You are fourteen years old, Samuel. You lost the man who was basically your father, along with his other sons, wicked as they were. You lost the ark, and now you are the only priest at Shiloh during Israel's darkest time since we fled Egypt.[215] And you say you *don't know what's wrong*? Sweetie, you are allowed to be sad. You are allowed to mourn Eli."

"I just don't know what to do, mom. What do I do?"

"I don't know, son," said Hannah. "But God has had plans for you ever since before you were born. He will help you through this."

"I know, I know," said Samuel. "I know."

The young man stood up, clearly attempting to put on a brave face. "How about I try on the coat?" he said through a forced smile.

Hannah stood up as well, her face still riddled with concern at the sudden outburst and equally sudden remission. Samuel put the coat on. It fit a loosely but was quite handsome, even on the lanky young man.

"It really looks great, if I do say so myself!" said Hannah. "It's a little big, but you have some growing left to do, don't you?"

---

[215] 1 Samuel 4

Samuel forced another smile and examined the coat as much as he could while it was on him. "It really looks good?" he said.

"Oh, yes. You look very handsome, Samuel! I think I'm getting better at this. Do you remember the first coat I ever brought you, eleven years ago? I guess you wouldn't. You were probably too young. Well, let's just say it didn't look quite as nice as that!"

A small smile, this one genuine, temporarily broke its way through Samuel's expression. "Stay right here, mom. I've got something to show you."

He left the room quickly and shortly returned with a tangled mass of clothing. He extracted from the bundle a coat, smaller than the one he was wearing, and placed it neatly on the ground. He withdrew another, still smaller, and placed it to the right of the first. Then he took out another, which was larger, and put it to the left. He continued this until eleven coats were placed on the ground, in a neat order with the smallest on the right going up to the largest on the left. As the coats got larger so did the detail and the skill that went into them. Finally, he took off the coat he was wearing and placed it all the way to the left of the line.

"You kept them all, every one of them! This is every coat I ever gave you, one for every year!"[216] Hannah smiled excitedly and moved closer to examine the row of garments. Twelve coats were laid out before her, a timeline of the life of her firstborn son.

She moved towards the first and smallest, placed all the way to the right. It was tiny by comparison to the others. It was yellow once, but now the color was faded and there were multiple holes in the garment. "Oh, look at this! You were so *little*! But these holes ... did Eli not have anyone who could patch these up? I guess it doesn't matter now."

She turned back to her son. In his eyes was a fresh welling of tears. She moved towards him and held him in her arms.

"Oh, my son," she said, pushing back the stray hairs threatening to find their way to her eyes. "I'm sorry, I didn't mean it that way. You really are a mess today, aren't you?"

Samuel attempted, again, to push away the sadness.

---

[216] 1 Samuel 2:19

After a moment, Hannah let her son go. She picked up the second largest coat, the one she'd brought him last year. It was also done in red and black, like the newest coat next to it. "Do you remember this one?" she asked.

"Yes, that's the one I had when dad—when Eli died."

"That was hard for you."

"He died so suddenly. They came to tell him that the ark was taken and that his sons Hophne and Phinehas were both killed, he just fell back in his chair and that was it. Even Phinehas' wife died. I lost my whole family in one day, and the ark too. Now I'm here, alone, at this empty Tabernacle."

"And what else?" said his mother.

"What?" said Samuel. "I don't know. That's it."

"That's not *it*. You had all those terrible things that happened. But what else happened? You've had this coat for a whole year."

"Um … I've got a new nephew, Ichabod. The day Phinehas died his wife had a son."[217]

"Oh, that's nice. What else?"

"I don't know, mom. That's all."

"Everything you've said happened in one day. There are a lot of other days in a year. What else happened?"

"I guess … lots of people came here, to give sacrifices or to seek a word from Yahweh. Yahweh gives me messages for them. I talked to some today, they were here only a few minutes ago."

"Oh? And what does Yahweh tell them?"

"Well, like, the people who came today were a father and mother. They had a sick child, and they wanted Yahweh to heal him. He told me that he would heal the boy and also give them more children, and that they should stop abusing their servants and animals."

"That sounds very good," said Hannah. "So, you've had a hard year. But even so, a lot of good has come from what you've done. Sick children are healed, and even lowly donkeys have peace and rest thanks to you."

"Thanks to Yahweh, not me. I'm only the messenger."

---

[217] 1 Samuel 4:20-22

"A very important job, and one few are chosen for!"

Hannah smiled at Samuel. He returned a smile of his own, but again it was forced and clearly for her benefit.

"Tell me," said Hannah, "which of these coats were you wearing when you first received a message from Yahweh?"

Samuel moved to the coat that was fourth from the left; the coat she'd made for him three years prior. This one was entirely black. There was considerable wear on the garment, and even one particularly large hole in one of the sleeves. He picked it up and presented it to his mother.

"It was this one," he said, as he handed it to Hannah. "I was sleeping in the Tabernacle. He called my name, but I'd never heard him before, so I thought it was dad—um, Eli. I went to Eli and asked him what he wanted. I think I woke him up. He told me to go back to bed. It happened two more times, and on the third time dad realized that it must be God. He told me to go and lie down and, when God called me again, to say, 'Speak, your servant is listening.' So that's what I did. That was the first time he ever spoke to me, the first message he ever gave me."[218]

"Wow," said Hannah. "You've never told me that before! That must have been amazing!"

"It was pretty amazing," admitted Samuel. "But the message was ... not good."

"What was it?"

Samuel hesitated. He had only ever told this to one person before, and even now that Eli was dead and it shouldn't matter anymore, he still wasn't sure he should talk about it. His mother only stared back patiently as he agonized over what to do.

"It was," he said finally, "a message about Eli and his family. He said he was going to judge Eli and his family for the terrible things his sons had done.[219] They were really bad, mom."[220]

"I know," said Hannah. "Everyone knows about *those* two."

"Yahweh said Eli should have stopped them, but he didn't. Eli made

---

[218] 1 Samuel 3:1-10
[219] 1 Samuel 3:11-14
[220] 1 Samuel 2:12-25

me tell him the next morning. I didn't want to tell him, but he made me. But even when I told him he didn't try to change. All he said was, 'He is Yahweh, let him do what seems right to him.'[221] I've never told anyone about this before, except for Eli."

"So ... you knew? You knew this was going to happen? You knew that Eli and his sons would die?"

"Yes, but God didn't tell me when."

Hannah looked again at the coat in her hands. "To think for almost three years you've had to carry that."

"No," said Samuel.

His mother looked questioningly at him.

"It ... it was actually a lot longer," said Samuel.

He gently took the coat from his mother and put it back in its place in the lineup. The he took another, this one fourth from the right. Seven years had passed since his mother had brought him this now-tattered yellow and red garment. The colors were faded and the material was thinning, but it still held its shape.

"This is when I first knew about Eli," said Samuel. He handed the coat to his mother who ran it through her fingers.

"But you said the first time Yahweh spoke to you was only three years ago?" asked Hannah.

"Yes, but he sent a messenger to dad and Hophne and Phinehas. I heard everything he said. He told them both Hophne and Phinehas would die in the same day, and that da—Eli's—entire family would be cursed."[222]

"So, you knew all this time?" said Hannah. "And they knew all this time? For seven years those two scoundrel sons of his knew the punishment for their sins was coming and they did *nothing*."

"Yes," said Samuel. "But mom, *everyone* is like that! They all come here, saying they are seeking Yahweh, but really they just want something. Everyone calls him God and Lord but then they turn around and continue doing the same things. Even Hophne and Phinehas only cared about women and respect and plenty of meat to eat."

---

[221] 1 Samuel 3:15-18
[222] 1 Samuel 2:27-34

"You paint a bleak picture, son," said Hannah. "But I don't think everyone is exactly like that."

"Maybe not. But so many are."

Samuel paused for a moment and watched his mother, who was still examining the old coat.

"There was something else, too," said Samuel. "Something else the messenger said."

"What did he say?" prompted Hannah.

"The messenger said Yahweh would raise up a faithful priest, who will do what he wants, and anyone left in Eli's house would come and beg him for a job.[223] He looked at me, mom. The messenger said, 'a faithful priest,' and looked at *me* when he said that."

Samuel looked worried and guilty, as if he'd just told some great secret that he'd been holding inside. His mother only waited, as if expecting more.

"Don't you see, mom? Don't you see? How can I live up to *that*? What if I can't do it? What if he gives up on me and turns his hand against me like he did with Eli's family? I can't do all of this! I can't be what God wants, and what all these people want and ... and what you want, mom! I can't do it. Someday, everyone will see it. They will all see what I am inside, that I'm not this perfect guy they think I am! I will fail and everyone will see what I really am and it will all be over!"

Samuel dropped his eyes, unsure of what his mother would say.

But Hannah only laughed. Samuel looked at her face questioningly and a little hurt. She tried to stifle the laughter but it was a few seconds before she was able to bring it to a close.

"I'm sorry," she said, "I'm sorry. I don't mean to laugh at you." She laughed again. "It's just ... *perfect*? Really, son? Have you not seen your reflection lately? The young man who stands before me can barely take care of his hair, and he's worried that people won't realize he's not *perfect*?"

Samuel couldn't help but crack a smile.

"Son, nobody thinks you are perfect, least of all Yahweh, who knows your heart better than you do. And do you think one failing

---

[223] 1 Samuel 2:35-36

would really be the end of all of it? You said he gave Eli and his sons *years* to repent, even though they were doing truly wicked things. He is patient and slow to anger. But justice and mercy demand that he stop men like Hophne and Phinehas from hurting his children. You know this!"

Samuel was silent; the silence of one who knows what he is hearing is true but doesn't want to admit it.

Hannah took the old coat and placed it back in line. Then she moved back to the farthest right one: the tiny, tattered yellow coat that barely held its shape. She picked it up carefully and turned back to Samuel.

"This thing is so small. It's funny, it's like it's from a different child; a child I remember but don't have anymore. In his place I have you. But you *were* this small once. This is the coat I made for you when I first brought you to Eli."

Hannah's eyes watered as she spoke.

"It hurt so much to leave you here. You cried so loudly. I felt as if I was betraying you. I didn't know how I could live without you. But I had to trust Yahweh, as much as it hurt. I cried for weeks afterwards."

Samuel remained silent. He didn't ask the question that came into his head: *Why* did you leave me here? Many past years' conversations had centered around exactly this question. Every explanation had been given and tears had been spent to exhaustion. There was no point in bringing it up again. Samuel knew that it had all somehow been a part of Yahweh's plan, and though he still struggled to accept it, there was no point in sullying his one chance to spend time with his mother rehashing that topic.

Hannah spoke again. "And I'll tell you this, the events that led to you being here certainly didn't come from some kind of perfect family. For years I was childless, but you already know that. What you don't know is that every year, just as we do now, we would come here to Shiloh for our annual sacrifice, and every year your father's other wife would taunt me and mock me for having no kids.[224] I would watch as a large portion of meat was dulled out to feed all her family but only a

---

[224] 1 Samuel 1:3-8

single serving was given to me. It was an annual reminder of my shame, and she never let the opportunity pass. And every year it was the same; she mocked me incessantly, and when I couldn't take it anymore, I would break down and cry and refuse to eat. Even that single serving I was given would go uneaten.

"But one year I took my brokenness and shame and brought it to Yahweh. I pleaded with him for a son—for you, my Samuel—and I promised that if he would give me just one son I would never cut his hair and he would be devoted to Yahweh forever. I was praying with such anguish that Eli thought I was drunk and almost kicked me out! But when I explained it to him, I remember exactly what he said: 'Go in peace, and may the God of Israel grant you what you asked.'[225]

"I couldn't believe it! Yahweh had told me he would grant my request! I went away so happy, and then finally ate something. And it wasn't long before exactly what he said came true, and you were born.[226] Years later, he gave me many more children.[227]

"And now, here you are. God took a shamed woman like me, and a broken family like ours, and even the sinful ways that we treated each other and turned them all into a tremendous blessing."

Hannah put the coat down. She moved closer to her son and held him by the shoulders, looking directly into his eyes.

"And that blessing," she continued, "was not just for our family, but for all of Israel. Because now you stand here at Shiloh, ministering to all of the people of Israel. Where once there were those wicked men Hophne and Phinehas, now there is someone who seeks after the heart of Yahweh. Where once there was the sin and curse whose fruit was the loss of the ark, now there is the seed of blessing. God has chosen you not because you are perfect but because you love him and seek his ways. This is a burden for you, but he will encourage and strengthen you and help you bear it, and bear it joyfully. And he will not turn his back on you or crush you should you ever fail. Like a good teacher he will patiently guide and direct you towards what is good and right, as he has been doing with all of us for as long as I can remember and

---

[225] 1 Samuel 1:9-18
[226] 1 Samuel 1:19-20
[227] 1 Samuel 2:18-21

much longer."

The complaints that were so readily at Samuel's lips were crushed under the weight of the grace and truth of his mother's statements. He only stared silently, uncomfortably close to his mother's face, until the situation grew awkward.

Finally, Hannah took a step back and smiled slyly. "Don't you normally get some kind of compensation for advice like what I just gave you? I'm really not sure what you are complaining about. This whole priest thing seems like a pretty easy gig! Now come on, we should get back out there with everyone else. There's much work to be done and you should catch up with the rest of the family, too."

Shortly the two were headed back. As soon as Samuel was sufficiently distracted by conversations between him and his siblings, Hannah pulled her husband aside.

"Listen," she said at a whisper, "I think you might want to consider finding that boy a wife sooner rather than later. He's a bit of a wreck."

Elkanah looked over his son, paying particular attention to the long, frazzled hair that seemed to have a mind of its own, or possibly more than one.

"I think you may be right," he said.

The Victorious Son of the Baggage King

See the pair of them striding with a determined air in the light of the rising sun: the prince and his armor bearer. Their resplendent glory is ... well, to be fair, it's more of a *perceived* resplendent glory.

They have the gait right. Chin up? Check. Shoulders back? Check. Steely-eyed determination? Check. A bit of dirt and grime, implying that these are not men afraid of getting their hands dirty or their swords bloody? Check.

But there are, to be sure, some problems. For starters, while they are probably perfectly willing to get their swords bloody, they will have to settle for just one bloody sword, since that's all they have between them. The prince has the sword, of course—surely he's due at least a *little* resplendent glory. He is a prince, after all.

The armor bearer has to make due with wielding a sickle. There are only two swords in the entire kingdom, and the other is currently in the hands of the king back at the camp.[228] A sickle lacks a certain nobility on the battlefield, but his enemies will learn shortly that ignoble weapons can still leave you very, very dead.

There is the problem of the armor as well. There simply isn't much of it. Still, to be called an armor bearer, one must presumably bear some armor, so the man is holding the prince's shield. The shield is simple and lacking considerably in the resplendent glory department.

Allow the mind's eye to turn away from this pair for a moment and focus in on the camp they left. It might at first seem impressive.

There is the king, tall and handsome, standing head and shoulders above everyone around him.[229] He is king Saul, the first king of Israel. He surveys the opposing army in a manner that is quite possibly noble, though a careful observer will note the well-hidden signs of uncertainty.

Six hundred battle-hardened soldiers are scattered in the camp

---

[228] 1 Samuel 13:19-22
[229] 1 Samuel 9:2

around him.[230] Despite their lack of weaponry, they are a hardy-looking bunch. They look to be the type of men who would prefer a broken finger to saying "mercy". This, it turns out, is because any man who wasn't incredibly brave or possibly foolhardy has already left and can either be found among the ranks of the enemies or hiding in a cave nearby.[231]

Turn towards the opposing army, the Philistines. Saul's ragtag group doesn't look so impressive now, does it? See those chariots? There are three thousand of them. See those soldiers? No one has even bothered counting them. That would probably require some new breakthrough in mathematics.[232]

The prince and his armor bearer are striding right towards that massive army.

It would at first appear that something very bad is about to happen to this armor bearer and his prince.[233] But the two men know something that no one else does, or at least that many others have forgotten.

~

"Palti! This food tastes like crap!"

"I'm sorry," said Palti. Palti was a bit out of sorts. Truthfully, the man was so often out of sorts that he probably didn't even remember what sorts looked like, but today was particularly bad. Defecting from the clearly-doomed Israelite army to the Philistines was bound to take its toll on any man, in sorts or out of them. And then there was that dream he kept having. "I told you I wasn't a chef, and anyway I don't have much to work with."

Palti served a wooden ladle full of piping-hot who-knows-what to the next soldier waiting in line. The soldier glared at it briefly, as if trying to decide whether to eat it or dump it out on the ground, but he

---

[230] 1 Samuel 13:15, 1 Samuel 14:2
[231] 1 Samuel 13:6-8
[232] 1 Samuel 13:5
[233] 1 Samuel 14:1

finally contented himself with a sneer and walked off, bowl in hand.

The one who had spoken first (who, it turns out, was the commander of the small forward outpost, though that information isn't terribly relevant since he'll be dead in a few minutes) continued, "What's in it?"

He prodded it with a spoon, prompting a jiggle to course through the strange almost-liquid. Once the movement had started, it didn't seem inclined to stop anytime soon.

"You probably don't want to know," said Palti. "Just eat it." Palti served another ladle-full to another waiting soldier and was rewarded with another sneer.

"Oh, gods, you Hebrews are a backwards bunch," said the commander. "I can't imagine why you're all being allowed to join us. It's not like we need the help."

"Don't worry, they don't even trust me with a sword. They have me cooking!" Palti spit in disgust. This is never a good idea when you are standing over an open pot. Fortunately, nobody seemed to notice.

"It's not like you had a sword before you came here," said the commander. "All you Hebrews coming at us with farm tools. Hah! What a joke! The baggage king and his farmer army!"

The twenty or so soldiers in the outpost laughed obediently. But one, a large fellow with eyes that showed all the depth and wisdom of the average cow, spoke up. "Baggage king, boss?"

"Yeah," said the commander, "the baggage king. Palti here told us all about it last night, didncha Palti? Said he was there at the, uh, coronation, if it can be called that. Why don't you tell us the story again, Palti?"

"Um, no thanks," said Palti.

"That's an order, Hebrew!" said the commander, with a sudden force that caused Palti to spill the current contents of his ladle onto the feet of the last soldier in line. As it happens, open-toed sandals provide very little protection against steaming hot liquid.

When the soldier had stopped swearing and his colleagues had stopped laughing, Palti began his story.

"It's just that," he said, "when the king was being selected by lot—"

"Ha ha, d'ya hear that boys? They choose their king at random. I'm sure nothing could go wrong there!"

"It's not random!" said Palti, a little more harshly than he'd intended. "It's, I mean, they're ... they're blessed by God. By Yahweh."

"Oh?" sneered the commander. "I didn't know he was so concerned with dice. Perhaps that's why I lost so much to Amog yesterday." The commander gestured to another soldier. "Hey, Amog, no fair—I didn't know you were using a *god*! That's cheating!"

The soldiers laughed again.

Palti unconsciously rubbed the grey piece of cloth tied to his arm just above the elbow, required by all Israelite defectors before they could join the ranks of the Philistine army. It itched a little.

"I'm so very sorry," said the commander in a voice dripping with sarcasm, "please continue your story, Palti."

"Well, when we had selected Saul—er, King Saul, that is—he wasn't there. So they asked God where he was, and God said he was hiding in the baggage. They pulled him out and stood him in front of everyone and made him king."[234]

"See?" said the commander. "The baggage king!"

"Hey, boss," said a soldier with a face like a bald weasel, "you shouldn't make fun of him. The god of the Hebrews might get you! Apparently, he's good for dice *and* baggage!"

There was another raucous round of laughter from Philistine soldiers. It may be comforting to know that this would be their last one.

Palti rubbed the cloth on his arm again. He was feeling extremely uncomfortable, and not just for the obvious reason that he was surrounded by men who would just as quickly kill him as they would any Israelite. It was the dream, that's what was getting to him.

He hadn't slept well in days. The dream haunted him. As soon as he got to sleep it would start again.

In his dream he saw the Philistine army filling the countryside like so many locusts ready to devour anything in their path. Then he saw the tiny remnants of the Israelite force—those who hadn't fled to the Philistines or the nearby caves. They looked pitiful and few. They

---

[234] 1 Samuel 10:20-25

didn't even have weapons.

The Philistines army, to a man, was laughing at the puny Hebrew force.

But then he saw something else. It was as if it suddenly appeared, except that it didn't appear. It was there all along, he was just suddenly able to see it: another army, vast and glorious. The soldiers gleamed so brightly it hurt the eyes to look at them. They carried weapons with such unique and intricate complexities, and with such definitive purpose, that a master craftsman could have spent his life trying to replicate just one of them without ever getting it quite right. Each soldier looked like he could hold against a thousand men, and yet there were so many that they dwarfed the Philistine army.

At the head of them all stood a figure like a man. He wore a crown on his head and his glory shown so brightly that the others looked dim by comparison. In the dream, Palti knew his name.[235] He knew it in that way that one knows things in dreams without being able to articulate it.

The crowned figure laughed. He looked at the Philistine army—he looked at *Palti*, standing among them—and he laughed. And then they charged.

It was always at this moment that Palti would wake up.

"Palti!"

Palti shook himself back to reality. The commander had been calling him for some time.

"Ha! You're a useless daydreamer and a terrible cook!"

"I told you," said Palti, "I'm not a cook."

"Oh, that's right, you wanted a sword, didn't you? Here, take mine!"

The commander tossed the sword to Palti, who fumbled for it, missed, stumbled backwards, and knocked over the remains of the substance that could generously be called "soup" onto the ground. He stood, picked up the sword, and held it shakily in his hands.

"All you gotta do is beat me," said the commander. "You have that sword. I have nothing. Surely you can beat me, right? If you do, I'll take you off cooking duty and you can serve in the ranks like a real man!"

---

[235] 1 Samuel 17:45 and many other places

The men around the camp smiled and found places to sit, preparing for the show.

Palti hefted the sword with a determined air. He stepped cautiously towards the commander.

"Uh, boss?" The voice came from a soldier looking out over the small cliff the outpost sat on.

"Not now! Can't you see I'm busy? This Hebrew here is going to show me how it's done!"

"Boss, you gotta see this."

With an exasperated sigh, the commander walked over to the edge of the cliff. The other men, including Palti, joined him.

There, walking towards them, or more accurately *striding* towards them, were two Israelites. They were nearly at the foot of the cliff-face. One had a sword at his side. The other had a sickle and carried a shield as well.

"Well, boys," said the commander, "will you look at that. The Hebrews are crawling out of their holes! Hey, you two! Why don't you come up here? Maybe we can teach *you* a lesson instead of Palti here!"[236]

The man with the sword said something to the other.

"What'd he say?" said the commander.

"I think he said something about Yahweh winning a battle even with only a few soldiers."[237]

"Ha! A few is right!"

Palti remembered his dream. "I think he's got more than a few," he said quietly, but none of the others seemed to notice.

The soldiers watched as the two men slowly climbed, using both their hands and feet.[238]

"Boss, you want us to just drop some rocks on them?"

"Nah, these two won't be a problem. Let them climb."

"But, boss, that one's got a sword."

"Well, what do you think that metal thing at your side is? A shovel?"

---

[236] 1 Samuel 14:1-12
[237] 1 Samuel 14:12
[238] 1 Samuel 14:13

"It's just that ... boss, I thought the Israelites didn't have any swords."

"The king does," said Palti. "And ... the prince. Jonathan."

The commander's eyes lit up. "Prince Jonathan? Oh, this is *perfect*! Everyone back up. I've got this one."

The soldiers, each of whom was feeling vaguely apprehensive but having a hard time figuring out exactly why, stepped back. Palti—who was feeling the same apprehension, except he was beginning to suspect he knew *exactly* why—stepped back quite a bit farther.

"They're almost here now," said the commander. "All right, it's time for some action!" he said, reaching for his sword.

It wasn't there. He cursed. He spun towards Palti.

"Palti! I need my sword!"

Palti tossed the sword towards the commander. It flew high and to the right. The commander's grasp just missed it and then it tumbled over the cliff's edge.

"Palti, you worthleAHHHHHH," were the commander's final words. Jonathan stood over the body, his now-bloody sword in hand, radiating a resplendent glory that simply couldn't be explained by anything about his person.

The soldiers each froze where they stood. The man behind Jonathan scrambled up the rest of the cliff, got to his feet, tossed the shield to Jonathan, and then pulled out the sickle. It gleamed in the morning light exactly like a humble sickle shouldn't.

At this point it would only be right for someone to yell, "Let's get 'em!" and then for the twenty soldiers to rush at the prince and his armor bearer.

"Let's get 'em!" yelled Jonathan, and the two rushed at the twenty soldiers.

The first one fell before the others had time to process what was happening. Then the spell was broken. A few of the more prepared soldiers charged at the two while the others ran to grab their weapons. Those first were dead within seconds, and soon the remaining were rushing all over the camp, some running towards the Hebrews and some running from them.

Palti watched in stupefied amazement as one man after another fell before sword and sickle. He unconsciously backed up as the fighting continued until he was at the very edge of the outpost.

Then they were all dead, every one of them, while the two Hebrews stood triumphantly amidst bodies scattered all over the place.[239]

The armor bearer signaled to Jonathan and pointed at Palti. Palti looked again at the grey cloth tied to his arm. "A traitor," said the armor bearer.

And then they charged.

Palti's vocal chords emitted a sound few men are capable of. He ran with everything he had. Fear infused his legs with speed and stamina previously unknown in his life. He bolted towards the main encampment, thinking that surely there amidst the countless Philistine soldiers he would be safe from these two raging maniacs. He tried very hard, and very unsuccessfully, not to think about the vision of the large and glorious heavenly army from his dream.

He could feel the two gaining on him. Panic gripped him and he ran even harder.

It seemed they were almost upon him when he entered the outskirts of the massive camp of the main army. He could swear he felt their breath on his neck.

He bolted into the camp screaming, "The Hebrews! The Hebrews!"

The soldiers nearby stood up.

Palti ran behind the nearest tent he could find and peeked around it.

Two raging Hebrews charging into the camp and killing everyone completely failed to materialize. There was simply no one there.

A man nearby came up to him. He had a serious air about him.

"What happened?" demanded the man.

"The ..." Palti struggled for breath. "The forward outpost! It's gone! They killed everyone! It happened so fast! They killed everyone!"

The last few nearby who weren't already devoting all of their attention to Palti began doing so.

"I'm the only one left!" Palti was almost yelling.

"Calm down," said the serious man. "How many were there?"

---

[239] 1 Samuel 14:13-14

"Um ... well ..."

"Didn't you see? Just an estimate is fine, but I need it fast!"

"Well, there were ... two."

Silence reigned for a moment. A man nearby said, "Two?"

"Two thousand, you idiot!" said another man. "Obviously it's not two, two men couldn't have taken an outpost on a cliffside! Two hundred, *maybe*, but they'd have to go around the cliff-face and then we would have seen them, and even the Israelites aren't stupid enough to attack us with only two hundred men! This poor man's out of breath, and the enemy is almost upon us. We don't have time for your stupid questions!"

"Thousand?" said Palti. "No, I mean—"

"Two thousand?" said the serious man. "They must have had a hidden force we didn't know about. I wonder how many there are. Take a minute and catch your breath. We need you ready to fight, they could be here any second! I've got to go tell the general."

The man ran off, shouting, "Prepare for battle! The Hebrews are attacking! Prepare for battle! The Hebrews ..."

The soldiers nearby scrambled to get themselves ready.

Almost immediately another man was at Palti's side. There was a grey cloth tied around his arm, just like Palti's; another defector.

"Listen," he said, "how bad is it, really?"

"Uh—" said Palti.

"It's just that," said the man, "we don't have a lot of time, see? And guys like you and me, we gotta make a choice. Just trying to survive, right?"

"Um—" said Palti.

"Here, come with me. Let's talk to the others."

The man pulled Palti by his unresisting hand. They passed by hurried soldiers and frantic activity until finally they came to a large tent. The man pushed Palti inside.

Multiple men were huddled together, each wearing the grey cloth on their arm that marked them as Hebrew defectors. They looked expectantly at Palti.

"Tell them," said the man. "We need to know who's going to win. We need to know what to do. Should we join back with the other

Hebrews or should we stay with the Philistines?"

Palti stood, stunned and completely unsure of what to say.

"Look, don't judge us!" said the man, misinterpreting Palti's silence. "You're a defector, same as us! We share the same fate! You're one of us! We've got families to provide for, see, we can't go around fighting battles for kings that have nothing to do with us!"

"Families?" said another man. "Gabran, what're you talkin' about? You're as single as a dead lion!"

"I might have a family, someday," snapped back the man identified as Gabran. "But not if these kings kill me first!"

Palti was finally recovering. "Listen," he said, "I don't think—"

"And what's going on in here?" This latest interruption was due to another soldier who had entered the tent, this one a native Philistine. Palti spun around to face him. "You lot are spies, aren't you? I knew it! That was the Hebrews' plan all along! That's why they stood there with only six hundred men but refused to surrender! It was all a ploy!"

The man drew his sword. It's point swayed mere inches from Palti's nose.

"Well," he said, "I'll put a stop to thi—ungh!"

He doubled over, hands grasping a particularly sensitive area of his body that had just had a rather unpleasant interaction with Gabran's foot. Gabran grabbed Palti by the arm and yanked him out of the tent.

"Take that cloth off, quick!" said Gabran, as he removed his own. Palti yanked at the cloth until he managed to untie it and it fell to the ground.

The other defectors poured out of the tent and began scattering in various directions. Grey cloths floated silently to the dirt below.

Then the Philistine came out of the tent as well. His face was still revealing a pain that he was desperately trying to control.

"You're gonna pay for that!" he shouted.

Gabran and Palti backed up a few steps as the Philistine advanced, his sword raised and poised to strike. He stepped over the scattered grey cloths lying on the ground. One stuck to his sandal and traveled with him a few steps.

The soldiers nearby began to take notice and moved in on the three.

"What's going on here?" shouted one of them.

Palti looked at the cloth stuck to the soldier's sandal, and then at the advancing soldiers, and was struck by a desperate inspiration.

"A Hebrew defector!" yelled Palti, in his best impression of a Philistine accent. "He was in that tent! They're attacking! Help!"

"What? I'm not a Hebrew!"

"A likely story," said another nearby soldier. "We can see your cloth right there on your sandal!"

"That's not mine!"

Swords were drawn. "No more of your filthy lies! You die here!"

More swords were drawn. "I know this man! He's no Hebrew!"

"Stand down or I'll gut you as well!"

"Ha! I'd like to see you try."

As the first blows were struck, Gabran was suddenly pulling at the stunned Palti. "Come on," he said, "time to go!"

They headed back in the direction they came from. Once out of the immediate vicinity of the scuffle, others who heard the nearby fighting began asking them what was going on, but they ignored them and kept moving.

They moved closer and closer to the edge of the camp. There were few soldiers still left here as they'd all gone towards the commotion in front of the tent of defectors.

Palti could see it now, the edge of the camp. Just a few more feet...

A large man gripped him by his arm in a manner that suggested his only escape option likely involved a limb and a socket parting ways. Gabran stopped, looked back, gave him what can only be described as a panicked shrug, and continued on alone towards the outer edge of the camp.

"What's going on over there? I hear fighting!"

"It's ... it's the Hebrews!" said the terrified Palti.

"What? They're attacking already?"

The man shouted to a nearby soldier standing beside a tent at the very edge of the camp, just as Gabran sprinted by. "They're attacking! Tell the men to get moving, double ti—"

It was at this precise moment that a humble sickle came the closest to resplendent glory that a sickle has ever dared aspire. The soldier Gabran had just passed dropped to the ground with a heavy thud. At the same time, Prince Jonathan knocked the fleeing Gabran to the ground.

The armor bearer stepped out from behind the tent and knelt down to retrieve the expertly-thrown sickle. Lying next to it was the soldier's sword, which seemed to catch his eye as well. He picked them both up, sword in one hand, sickle in the other. His eyes briefly gazed from one to the other in consideration before he tossed the sword aside with a contented smirk.

He held up the sickle and gave Palti and the Philistine a smile that could have frozen a fire.

Jonathan emerged from behind him, dragging along a flailing Gabran.

Palti tried to tug away from the large man, but he may as well have tried beating a mountain in an arm-wrestling contest. The man barely seemed to notice him. He was staring, dumb-founded, at the two Israelites.

They approached slowly and purposefully. The armor bearer wielded the sickle in a manner that made Palti feel very much like a fully-grown grain plant.

The protesting Gabran was tossed to the ground in front of Jonathan. Gabran sat on the ground, bewildered and terrified, seemingly unsure of what to do next.

The fighting behind Palti, where he'd fled from the tent of defectors, was growing louder and more chaotic.

He heard the Philistine's panicked whisper, "They're ... they're everywhere!"

And that's when the earth shook.[240]

Starting slow, barely at the edge of the senses, and then building until its tremendous force was undeniable is precisely what it didn't do. This wasn't a standard earthquake. It wasn't required to go through the usual build up and release. It simply *was*. One second the ground stood still, the next it shook as if a nearby herd of elephants had just been told about a sale on peanuts.

The large Philistine almost fell over, but did not release his iron grip

---

[240] 1 Samuel 14:15

on Palti's arm. Sharp pain signals were sent to Palti's brain, where they were promptly ignored because his brain felt it was already dealing with enough as it was.

While the ground shook, Jonathan and his armor bearer merely stood. Palti could swear they were *smiling*.

Then the earthquake was over, just as quickly as it started.

The grip on Palti was released, causing his nearly-numb arm to tingle. The Philistine bolted, screaming at the top of his lungs, "Retreat! *Retreat!*"[241]

Jonathan chased after him, but the armor bearer stayed behind. He glared at Gabran. He glared at Palti.

"I think," he said, his words slow and casual, "if Yahweh wants to, he can destroy this entire Philistine army with just Jonathan. You two should choose a side, and choose wisely."

Then he was gone, following after Jonathan at a run. Suddenly Palti and Gabran were alone. Gabran got up and dusted himself off, neither of which was a simple endeavor after the events of the past couple of minutes. The shouting and sounds of battle seemed to be coming from everywhere in the camp now, but they were slowly getting farther and farther away.

"Where is the rest of the army?" said Gabran.

"There is no rest of the army. It's just those two."

"Ah. I was beginning to suspect. So ... the outpost?"

"All dead."

Palti thought an appropriate reaction would be surprise. But it seemed Gabran had had enough of surprised for a little while and opted for thoughtful instead.

"Two men killed an entire fortified outpost," said Gabran. "Maybe that armor bearer is right. We'd better make sure we are on the right side. Come on, let's gather as many other defectors as we can and tell them to join the battle."[242]

"What?" said Palti, incredulity creeping into his voice. "I don't care how good they are, there's only two! They can't *win*!"

Gabran only stared at him in silence while the battle sounds in the

---

[241] 1 Samuel 14:16
[242] 1 Samuel 14:21

encampment provided the most convincing counter-point any debater could hope for.

Finally, he said, "Look, you saw! The Philistines are fighting *themselves* now! They're scared and confused.[243] And with that earthquake, I don't blame them. Apparently, we really do have God on our side! Now is the time to strike! Anyway, King Saul and the rest of the men will soon realize what's going on and join in. We'll have every Hebrew for miles around chasing these Philistines![244] This could be our chance to crush them for good!"

Palti looked longingly at the open land just beyond the edge of the camp. He was so close to freedom.

Gabran seemed to notice and said, "Fine. I'll go gather the others by myself."

Gabran picked up the sword of the soldier who'd died of acute sickle poisoning and set off at a run.

For another brief moment, Palti considered following him. But then, with a shake of his head and a hardening of his heart, he ran towards the edge of the camp.

He tripped.

He fell.

~

Palti saw the Philistine army, as if from somehow overhead in the sky, or on the ground and zooming through them at uncanny speed, or both, or neither. They filled the countryside like a horde of locusts.

He saw the tiny remnant of the Hebrew army. They were anxious and scared. Poor farmers had to make due for trained soldiers. Plowshares, picks, axes, and sickles had to make due for swords and spears.

The Philistines laughed at the Israelites.

Suddenly there was something else. It didn't appear, it was there all along, but it was as if Palti's eyes were suddenly capable of seeing it. It

---

[243] 1 Samuel 14:20
[244] 1 Samuel 14:20-23

was the vast and glorious army of heaven. It surrounded the Israelite camp, an impenetrable wall of countless soldiers, each one wielding a weapon of indescribable beauty and unmistakable purpose and each one looking like he was very sure how to use that weapon.

At their head stood a figure like a man. He shone like the sun, as if even the light was afraid of him and running to get away. He wore a crown on his head with the kind of intricate detail that would make a fractal jealous.

Palti knew his name. He was the lord of heaven's armies.

The man looked at the Philistine army and he laughed. Then his face became serious, and with one command the entire heavenly army charged in perfect unison.

Palti was standing among the Philistines in the path of the heavenly army. He looked in panic at those around him, but none were reacting. It was like they didn't even know what was going on. They continued on eating, drinking, chatting, and generally doing the many other mundane tasks that people typically don't do when a powerful force is seconds away from destroying them.

The first few Philistines fell. Those around Palti began to take notice.

More fell. The Philistines grew restless.

Even more fell. The panic started. Philistines ran in every direction, some of them even *towards* the very army that was destroying them. There was confusion everywhere. Some of the Philistines were fighting each other. The army of heaven crushed any soldier it encountered as if stepping on a harmless ant.

Palti saw them growing closer, closer, ever closer. He closed his eyes. He fell backwards until he was sitting. He waited for death.

He waited a little longer for death.

He waited a bit more. Death sure seemed to be taking its sweet time.

Okay, seriously, death, thought Palti. *What's the deal here? You've got one job to do. I haven't got all day. I'm about to die, after all.*

He chanced opening his eyes. An endless wave of glorious warriors rushed past him, but most pressing was the sword. Where it was pressing, specifically, was against his chest. He followed a blade like metallic lightning up to a hilt of solid diamond to a hand that could crush worlds and up to a face like a supernova. Atop the head was a crown.

The lord of heaven's armies said, "Palti, you cannot serve two masters. Choose now whom you will serve!"[245]

~

Palti woke up.

He wasn't sure at first how he felt about that. On the one hand, he was still alive and no one was threatening him with immediate death by supernatural sword, at least not that he could see. On the other hand, he had a splitting headache from where his head had smacked against the tent peg when he'd tripped and fallen.

The sun overhead told him it was about midday. He'd been out for hours.

He got to his feet slowly, just in case he didn't have them anymore. Nope, they were fine. Legs, hands, arms, torso ... everything seemed to be more-or-less in working order. This was more than could be said for the soldier nearby with the sickle wound.

He stumbled inward of the camp. An eerie silence reigned. Here and there were cooking fires burned down to ashes, some with blackened meals still affixed above them.

It wasn't long before he saw the first body, and then another, and then another. Dead Philistine soldiers littered the encampment like a swarm of locusts after the vegetation has run out. The sights were gruesome, but truthfully nothing that the average adult Israelite man like Palti hadn't seen before.

His haze slowly lifted as he made his way through the camp. Food and water—that was the first thing. Those were easily obtained. Supplies were everywhere, guarded only by the dead.

After gathering a few morsels and some rather promising-looking wine, he sat down on a patch of earth with nothing too terribly unsightly in his immediate field of view. He ate and drank.

The dream kept nagging at him. He'd had it over and over again

---

[245] Matthew 6:24, Luke 16:13

ever since this mess with the Philistines had started but it had never gone that far before. It always ended with the heavenly army's charge. He never saw the man face to face like that. He never saw the sword up close. He was never threatened *personally*.

And what is it that this ... this ... lord wanted him to do exactly? Why tell him now? The Philistines were all gone or dead. And why should this guy care about Palti anyway? Palti was pretty sure it was important people like kings who were supposed to get messages like this, not lowly sold—er, defec—er, whatever it was that Palti was now. That is the prime benefit of being lowly: nobody cares too much what you do as long as long as you don't get in their way.

Still ... that man ... that face ... that *sword*. Palti didn't want to be on the wrong side of that sword. And that's what the man had made it sound like: like you had to choose, like there was no middle ground.

There are those sufficiently adept at rationalizing and sufficiently enslaved to their own desires who, upon hearing Palti's tale, would immediately begin questioning the right of this lord to make a claim that there were only two paths, only two sides. Could not some middle ground be found where small injustices go unanswered for the sake of my own safety? Could not a little bit of cruelty continue, so long as it isn't happening to me? Could I not, perhaps, serve God one day a week but then serve Myself the rest of the week?

Palti, however, had the advantage of not being so philosophically minded and also having been the one to *actually* see the man. To his mind, there was no mistaking this truth: there were only two sides and one of them contained the point of that sword.

So, he reasoned, there was nothing for it. Perhaps it was simply his full stomach now giving him courage, or perhaps he really was just more afraid of God than the Philistines. Whatever the reason, he got to his feet and began moving in the direction of the Philistines' retreat, under the assumption that if there was still fighting going on that's where it would be.

He picked up a decent-looking sword off a fallen Philistine in a half-hearted manner. Lowly Palti was off to glorious battle. Or, something anyway, probably glorious.

~

Glorious battle, it turned out, was somewhat hard to find. Palti had been unconscious for quite a while, and during that quite a while the Israelites had been chasing the Philistines at considerable speed.

He followed the tracks—not a terribly difficult process when pursuing an army—and there were periodic signs he was gaining on them; the blood looked fresher, the Philistine corpses as if they hadn't been that way as long. But still the rest of the day past and not a single glorious battle took place, at least not one involving Palti.

As evening threatened to turn into night, he could see that he was getting very close. He was even beginning to hear them.

He cautiously approached what would turn out to be the main Israelite force. King Saul and Prince Jonathan stood atop a small hill, visible more by torchlight than the sun, with the rest of the soldiers all in one large group.

Palti expected to see a celebration. Judging by the countless dead enemies Palti had seen on his journey—and indeed, there is nothing for judging the outcome of a battle like countless dead enemies—the Israelites had won a great victory today. There should have been eating, drinking, counting of plunder, and all manner of other things that a soldier might be inclined to do after a long day of not getting killed.

Palti edged his way through the throng of soldiers until he was nearly to the front. He glanced to his right and found to his mild horror that he was standing directly next to the armor bearer.

The armor bearer gave him a brief glare and then said, matter-of-factly, "The traitor." Mercifully, he didn't speak too loudly. Palti wondered if anyone else heard him, until he realized that this group—which had grown much larger than six hundred men now—was certain to contain plenty of other ex-defectors. Surely all would be forgiven after a day like today. Probably. Maybe.

The king seemed angry, and this anger was directed at Jonathan. This puzzled Palti. The man had single-handedly sent an entire army running. Well, to be fair, he used two hands, in quite a creative and disturbing manner at times. And of course there was that armor bearer of his who also had two hands and also seemed to know exactly how to use them. And then there was the entirety of heaven's army. But if you didn't count the heavenly army and the sickle-crazed armor bearer—oh, and the earthquake, mustn't forget that—and, finally, Jonathan's *other* hand, then he defeated an entire army single-handedly.

Jonathan was also the king's son. There are many benefits to being the king's son. Presumably one of them is that small offenses and even minor crimes are often overlooked.

So Palti listened in horrified fascination to find out what Jonathan could have possibly done to warrant the king's anger on a day like today.

"I tasted a little honey," said Jonathan. "I wasn't even there when you gave the command not to eat, how could I have known? Will you sentence me to die over honey?"[246]

"Yes!" raged the king. "You must die. May God strike me and kill me if you live!"[247]

Palti turned to the armor bearer.

"What?" he said. "He's sentenced to death?"

"Yes."

"For eating honey?"

"Yes."

The king ordered the elite soldiers of his personal guard to capture and bind Jonathan. Their reaction was roughly equivalent to that which comes in response to being told to wrestle a tiger.

"*Honey?*"

"Yes."

"But he ... and you ... and then the Philistines ... and so many dead ... and the sickle ... and ... and ... *honey?*"

"Yes."

The king now resorted to threats. His personal guard slowly advanced on Jonathan. Each of them seemed to be trying to stand slightly behind each other one of them.

"Aren't you going to do something?" Palti was nearly panicking now, and it was all the worse with the armor bearer's calm responses.

---

[246] 1 Samuel 14:43
[247] 1 Samuel 14:44

The armor bearer turned towards Palti and said, simply, "Choose a side."

Palti saw the king. *Gosh, he really is tall, isn't he?* he thought. *And that personal guard of his ... impressive men, they are. And there sure are a lot of soldiers under his command. And so many more of them have proper swords now ...*

But then he looked at the humble sickle at the armor bearer's side. And he thought about that glorious sword in the hands of the lord of heaven's armies.

The sickle was almost worse.

The advancing guard were growing braver, a fact which probably had something to do with Jonathan showing no signs of resisting them.

Palti sprang to his feet and ran to the top of the hill. He stood in front of Jonathan. The surprise on the face of the guards was quickly replaced with a devious grin. Jonathan was concerning—they'd seem him in action too many times to underestimate him—but this man that stood in front of them now was little more than a bit of sport.

"We can't do this!" shouted Palti.

The guard moved closer.

"Think about what he's done today! Look at this great victory we've won! Jonathan is a hero! Yahweh used him to defeat an entire *army*!"[248]

The guard moved even closer.

Suddenly, the armor bearer was by his side, bloody sickle at the ready.

The guard paused.

"As surely as Yahweh lives," said the armor bearer, "not one hair on his head will be touched."

Gabran emerged from the ranks of the assembled soldiers and joined them. Judging by the condition of his sword, even he'd found opportunity to use it. He stood next to the armor bearer and embedded the sword in the ground in front of him.

"God has helped him do a great deed today," said Gabran. "Should he die? Far from it!"

---

[248] 1 Samuel 14:45

The Victorious Son of the Baggage King

Another soldier joined them. Then another. The number of the defenders of Jonathan grew, first one or two at a time, then in small groups, and then in large groups, until Palti felt like the entire army was standing between Saul and his son.

In frustrated tones with a slight hint of relief, the king said, "Fine! But we cannot chase the Philistines any longer because of what Jonathan has done. We will rest here for tonight, and tomorrow we will gather the plunder and head home."[249]

Palti breathed, a thing which he only just realized he hadn't been doing.

Slowly, the soldiers disbanded, heading out to find whatever shelter they could to get through the rest of the night. Palti stood for some time as the anxiety slowly leaked out.

When he finally felt more like himself, he turned to Jonathan, but he was already gone, along with almost all the rest of the soldiers. So he turned back to the armor bearer, who seemed preoccupied with his sickle.

"It must be tough having a father like that," said Palti, with a nudge to the armor bearer.

The armor bearer hardly seemed to notice. He was still thoughtfully considering the sickle.

"I mean, seriously, what does he have to do to please the man, am I right?" said Palti, in a thinly veiled attempt at camaraderie.

The armor bearer turned the sickle over in his hands.

"But hey," continued Palti, "at least we have something to look forward to, eh? A man like Jonathan will make a fine king someday. If he lives that long, anyway."

The armor bearer seemed to reach a decision. "I no longer need this," he said. He placed the sickle into Palti's unresisting hands and walked off into the night without another word.

It was rude, but Palti was much too tired and relieved to be offended by anything short of a knife to the neck.

He examined the sickle in his hands in a manner that he hoped was a reasonable facsimile of reverence. He held it up in the moonlight to

---

[249] 1 Samuel 14:46

get a better view. The gravity of the situation slowly sank in. This was it; this was his *weapon*! The glorious sickle of Prince Jonathan's armor bearer, which felled so many Philistines in a single day that—

The handle snapped in two and the remains of a shoddily-crafted sickle fell to the ground.

"What a piece of junk!"

The Jailer

Orestes patrolled the hall of his prison in a slow parade of power, with his two guards trailing behind. Each authoritative thud of his boots was a reminder to his prisoners that he was outside of the cells, they were inside, and he intended to keep it that way. His sword hilt shimmered in the dim torchlight. His guards wore hard and emotionless expressions. His keys jingled.

The jingling keys was the part he liked best. His guards and boots and sword might have served to keep a single prisoner or two in check, but it was the keys that allowed him to stand as the immovable force, the unquestionable authority, the indomitable king of this tiny castle where all the subjects would happily toss him into one of the cells if given a chance. Outside of the prison he was just another Macedonian soldier, but in here he was emperor. A jailer is nothing without his keys.

Of course, much of it was an act. Resolute authority is a requirement for a jailer. It was for the sake of survival, not pride, that he reminded the prisoners who was in charge around here. Any weakness shown could be exploited, and soon he could be lying dead at the hands of a prisoner or watch helplessly as they all escaped. The latter was much worse. If a prisoner killed him, he'd at least do it quickly; the Roman government may not be so kind.

And so, he made a point of regular rounds like this. He took his time walking past each cell, reminding each prisoner individually of their place and his place.

He finished his walk around the outer cells and moved to the room with the inner cell. He hated it here. It terrified him, though he would never admit it. The large cell was so dimly lit the prisoners inside could barely see each other. This is where all the worst ones were. They lined the walls with feet chained securely.

One of them spoke. "Oh, hey boss man, those are some real shiny keys!"

Orestes and the two guards with him merely walked by the cell in silence as the prisoner continued.

"You don't suppose you could use those shiny keys and let me out? I've been talking with the other nice gentlemen—"

"Shut up, moron."

"—and they were telling me they wouldn't mind a bit. It would be all of our little secret."

Orestes carefully controlled his pace and gave no response.

"Yeah, you're a hard man, I can see that!" continued the prisoner. "But I know inside of you there's some compassion. You wouldn't let a guy just rot in here? I'm innocent you know."

"Shut *up*!" shouted another prisoner. "Boss, you can't leave us in here with Alphaeus. He's been doing this all evening!"

Orestes said nothing. He was nearly finished walking through the room.

The talkative prisoner identified as Alphaeus continued, "Oh, come on, really, boss? Is that supposed to scare us? You walking all slow and tough. 'Hey, look at me, Mister Boss Man, I've got the keys! I'm not scared at all of these *very dangerous prisoners* in my care, 'cause I've got the keys!' Perhaps we get out of here some other way, and then teach you a lesson before we leave, eh?"

He chuckled and looked around at the other prisoners for support, but all he received was another, "Shut up."

The younger of Orestes' guards, a slim-built man named Demetrios, turned towards Alphaeus. "Or perhaps you have a little *accident* tonight and never walk out of this prison again? Would you like that or would you rather close that big mouth of yours?"

Orestes placed his arm behind the young guard, out of sight of the prisoners, and tugged lightly on his shirt to indicate he should keep moving.

Once they were out of the room with the inner cell and out of sight of the prisoners, Orestes turned with sudden rage at the younger of his two guards.

"What do you think you were doing in there?" he said. "What did I tell you?"

"Sir, *someone* needs to teach that Alphaeus a lesson!" said Demetrios.

Orestes moved within inches of the young man's face. "You do not respond to them! You do not get angry, you do not show compassion, you do not show curiosity, you do not react in *any* way! You are not a man, not to them! You are a *force*! A man can be killed! Do you want to be killed?"

Demetrios held Orestes' gaze briefly, but was given no reprieve. He turned to the other guard—an older man named Koinos—for some support, but received none. Finally, he dropped his eyes. "Sorry, sir. It won't happen again, sir."

"Good," said Orestes. His tone softened. "I don't want to be killed either."

They became aware of a commotion outside that had been growing in volume unnoticed by them until now. Shouting from various voices could be heard.

Orestes moved towards the outer door. Just before he arrived there was a heavy knocking. He opened the door to the slowly fading light of the late day.

In front of him was one of the city magistrates, and behind him was a large crowd centered around two men stripped almost naked.[250] By the looks of it, they had been beaten severely only moments before. They looked as if they could barely stand. Fresh bruises were on every part of their body and blood was still oozing from the places where the skin had not been able to withstand the blows.

Whoa, thought Orestes, *what did these guys do?*

The city magistrate spoke as if in answer. "These men have been advocating for customs contrary to Roman law."[251] Various men in the crowd seemed pleased at his words.

Orestes noted that exactly which law was broken was carefully excluded from the statement. No surprises there. Unless you were a Roman citizen, the magistrates could do whatever they wanted with you.

"They are very dangerous," continued the magistrate. "I want them locked up securely. I don't need to remind you that your job and your very life may be forfeit should you lose any prisoners."[252]

---

[250] Acts 16:23-24
[251] Acts 16:20-21
[252] Acts 12:19

"No, sir, I am well aware," said Orestes, with a furtive look at the two men who seemed closer to falling over than to escaping from a cell. It was then that he noticed their faces. Something about them was ... off.

"Excellent," cried the magistrate in mock approval. "These men are under your care now. In the morning I will send further instructions."

Someone nearby thrust a small bundle of clothes into his hands, no doubt what the men were wearing before they were stripped and beaten.

"Very well, sir," said Orestes in a distracted tone. He handed the clothes to Koinos and then motioned for him and Demetrios to take hold of the men. He couldn't stop looking at their faces. They looked exhausted and pained, but something was missing, or perhaps something had been added. They should have been afraid, but they weren't afraid. In fact, they looked almost content. One of them radiated an authority that somehow maintained itself through the blood and bruises and despite the lack of clothes.

The two guards took hold of the men, in a display that Orestes was pleased to note appeared rough to the crowd and the magistrate without actually being so. They led them into the dark interior. Orestes gave a brief farewell and then shut the outer door and walked back with the men to the inner cell.

"I'm surprised to see these two in here," said Demetrios as they walked.

"What do you mean?" asked Orestes. "Do you know them?"

"You don't recognize them?" asked Demetrios.

"I don't think I'd recognize my own brother after a beating like that."

"They are the ones Dimnos' slave girl has been following around."

"Hmm. Wonder what happened that everyone suddenly turned on them like that."

Orestes, like everyone else in Philippi, knew all about what had been happening for the last few days.[253] A man in the city named Dimnos had acquired a slave girl a couple of years back, and it had

---

[253] Acts 16:12

turned out to be the best investment he'd ever made. The girl had some sort of spirit that could predict the future. Everything she said came true, and everyone in the city knew about it. Dimnos made a fortune charging people to hear predictions about themselves.[254]

But for the last three days she'd been doing nothing but following around this group of foreigners—Jews—and shouting the exact same phrase, over and over, until everyone in Philippi could have repeated it word-for-word: "These men are servants of the Most High God! They are proclaiming to you the way of salvation! These men are servants of the Most High God! They are proclaiming to you the way of salvation! These men are servants of the Most High God! They are proclaiming to you the way of salvation!"[255]

As they continued walking, Demetrios seemed thoughtful. "Salvation," he said. "What do you suppose that actually means?"

Much to Orestes' surprise, one of the prisoners they were escorting responded, "Salvation from the death that is the wages of our sin."

Another thoughtful moment passed as the group continued walking closer to the inner cells.

"Death?" asked Demetrios. "You mean like you won't die?" Normally Orestes would have been angry with the young man again, but his curiosity was also getting the best of him.

"Yes," said the prisoner. "God, the Most High God, the only true God and Lord of everything, sent his only son, Jesus, to the Jewish people to proclaim this salvation to them. His coming was foretold long ago in our scriptures.[256] He performed many miracles to prove who he was, and then he taught the people the way of God. Blind men were made to see,[257] lame men jumped up and leapt for joy,[258] and he even raised the dead.[259] He was killed on a cross by our own elders and leaders, but

---

[254] Acts 16:16
[255] Acts 16:17
[256] Deuteronomy 18:14-22, Psalm 16:9-11, Psalm 22, Isaiah 7:14-16, Isaiah 52:13-53:12, Daniel 2:44-45, Daniel 7:13-14, Daniel 9:20-27, Zechariah 9:9, and many more
[257] Mark 8:22-26, Mark 10:46-52, Matthew 9:27-31, John 9
[258] Matthew 9:2-8, Mark 2:1-12, Luke 5:17-26 John 5:1-15
[259] Luke 7:11-17, Luke 8:40-56, John 11:1-46

three days later he rose to life again,[260] just as he said he would.[261] His sacrifice was for the sin of all people. Now he is alive, and sin and death are beaten. We—and many others—are witnesses of these things. And God was not satisfied with only proclaiming this message to the Jews.[262] Jesus has sent us here to proclaim it to you and to all your people.[263] Believe in the Lord Jesus, and you will be saved."

They were now very close to the inner cell. None of the group said a word as they approached. Orestes opened the doors, and the two guards began chaining the prisoners against the wall.

"Hey, you're just going to leave these guys like this?" yelled the all-too-familiar voice of Alphaeus.

Orestes shot a warning glare towards Demetrios, lest he forget to remain quiet.

"Seriously?" shouted Alphaeus. "These guys are still bleeding. You aren't going to clean them up or something?"

Orestes was pleased to see that the young guard made no reaction. The last of the chains was locked while Alphaeus continued his protests to deaf ears.

When the three were once again out of earshot of the inner cell, Demetrios spoke up. "Sir," he said, "why aren't we cleaning up the wounds? They could be in real trouble if we don't take care of them."

Koinos responded before Orestes had a chance to. "You saw the magistrate, didn't you? He's a mean one. Apparently, he wants these two to suffer and he's going to notice if we tend to the wounds. If we want to keep our jobs, we'd best do what he wants."

"But they didn't even say what they did wrong!" said Demetrios. "You heard those men, babbling crazy stuff like that, they probably just ticked off the wrong guy."

---

[260] Matthew 26:47-28:20, Mark 14:43-16:8, Luke 22:47-24:53, John 18:1-21:25
[261] Matthew 12:39-40, Matthew 16:1-4, Matthew 16:21, Matthew 17:9, Matthew 17:22-23, Matthew 20:17-19, Matthew 26:26-29, Matthew 27:62-64, Mark 8:31-38, Mark 9:9-10, Mark 9:30-32, Mark 10:32-34, Mark 10:45, Mark 14:22-25, Luke 9:21-27, Luke 9:31, Luke 9:43-45, Luke 11:29-32, Luke 13:31-35, Luke 18:31-34, Luke 22:14-20, John 2:18-22, John 6:43-58, John 10:14-18, John 12:20-36, John 14:1-30, John 16:16-33, John 17:11-13
[262] Isaiah 49:6
[263] Acts 9:15-16

"Crazy stuff, huh?" asked Koinos.

"Yeah. You heard him. God Most High or Jesus or whatever he was talking about."

"But what about Dimnos' girl?"

"What about her?"

"She's never been wrong before."

The three arrived at their small table and chairs where so much of their shifts were spent. No sooner had they sat down than they heard the singing.

"Who's that?" asked Koinos.

"I think it's the newcomers," said Orestes.

"They're singing!?"

"It would appear so."

"Let me guess: more stuff about God."

"Yup, sounds like it."

"Well, at least they have decent voices."

The two noticed young Demetrios. He appeared to be quietly counting to himself.

"What're you doing?" asked Koinos.

"I'm betting forty-five seconds."

"Forty-five seconds until wha—oh, Alphaeus."

The three waited patiently as the young guard counted. The clear and simple song continued on. Forty-five came and went.

"Nothing," said Koinos.

"Give it a bit longer."

They waited again. Still nothing could be heard but the two men singing.

"I thought for sure we'd hear him," said Demetrios, almost complaining. "Alphaeus *never* shuts up, but he's quiet for these two?"

"Maybe they really are sent by God," said Koinos in an attempt at a joking tone. The three chuckled nervously.

Orestes briefly began to wonder if he shouldn't have cleaned the wounds after all. But his guard was right; doing so would get on the bad side of a city magistrate, and that's a dangerous place to be.

The three settled in at the small table for the evening. Minutes turned into hours as they played games, chatted, and did the occasional round. All the while the two prisoners never stopped singing and praying.[264] In a profession where long hours of boredom are the norm, the singing prisoners were a welcome distraction.

After sunset they extinguished most of the torches so the prisoners could sleep. Even after it was nearly pitch-black in the inner cell, the two new prisoners continued singing. The others only listened, without a word.

The guards began their usual custom of sleeping in shifts. Orestes always insisted on two men being awake, so that if anyone got drowsy there would be someone around to keep him from accidentally falling asleep.

Koinos had the first sleeping shift. He was always better able to get sleep early in the night than Orestes or Demetrios. The other two continued playing games and chatting to pass the time. Even now, after all this time, the singing and praying continued. The effect it had on the prisoners was amazing. Orestes had never seen them so quiet and, oddly, content.

Orestes' turn to sleep came. He settled into the mat he had on the floor against the wall and closed his eyes ...

It felt like he had no sooner fallen asleep than something woke him back up. His sleep-addled brain couldn't process what was happening. His thoughts moved slowly, but eventually he realized some sort of earthquake was happening. For a moment he pondered just going back to sleep.

But then the earthquake stopped, and as it did a loud metallic symphony echoed throughout the building. Orestes recognized the sound, even though he'd never heard so many of them at once: it was the sound of chains being unlocked and cell doors being opened.[265]

The fog in Orestes' sleepy mind instantly evaporated. He sprang to his feet and instinctively reached for his sword hilt. He took two steps towards the nearest empty cell, but then the futility of his situation struck him.

Every single cell in the prison was opened, and by the sound of it every chain was released. Either the prisoners had somehow already

---

[264] Acts 16:25
[265] Acts 16:26

escaped—Had he been asleep that long? Surely he would have heard something?—or perhaps they were all still in there. Orestes wasn't sure which was worse.

If the prisoners were still in there, in a few seconds they would be bursting out of their empty cells. Orestes, Koinos, and Demetrios wouldn't stand a chance against them. They would be dead within minutes.

But if the prisoners weren't in there, if they had escaped, then it was the Romans Orestes would have to answer to. They wouldn't kill him quickly, like the prisoners would. Instead of being dead in minutes it would take hours, or more likely days, as his body pinned to a cross slowly weakened until he couldn't hold it up any longer ...

No. No. He'd made up his mind about this a long time ago. He'd had too many close calls in his career and seen too many executions on a cross to let that happen to him. No, they weren't going to take him alive. At least if he did it himself it would be quick.

He drew his blade.[266] This is a moment he'd never spoken to others about but nevertheless planned in great detail. His resolve needed to be strong. He couldn't delay or he would soon be in the hands of the prisoners. He placed the blade towards his chest and held the hilt with both hands. Sweat began beading on his forehead. His heart raced. He wanted a way out, but he knew there was no way out. He'd determined long ago how he should do this if the time came. He looked at the ground. *Just fall*, he thought, *that's all you have to do. Just fall forward.* He took a deep breath. *Do it quick before the prisoners come. Keep the sword perfectly steady. Don't do it half-heartedly; finish the job or you won't be able to.* He prepared to tilt forward—

"Stop!"[267] The voice came from the inner cell, out of sight from Orestes. "We're all here. We aren't escaping. Don't harm yourself!"

Orestes halted. He carefully lowered his sword and looked around. It was true. The prisoners should have reacted by now, but no one had moved.

"Lights!" called Orestes to the guards.[268] As he did so, he turned,

---

[266] Acts 16:27
[267] Acts 16:28
[268] Acts 16:29

and found that shouting was unnecessary. Demetrios stood only a few feet away, staring at him, apparently having witnessed Orestes' entire incident with the sword. Orestes looked down at the weapon, still in his hand, and carefully sheathed it.

"Lights, I said," said Orestes, still urgently, but this time in a calmer tone. The young guard sped off to light the torches just as Koinos started doing so as well.

Orestes rushed towards the inner cell. When he arrived, he saw the two new prisoners simply standing. Around them all of the prisoners sat terrified in exactly the place where they had been chained to the wall, despite the chains having been removed. Even Alphaeus didn't so much as move or speak. Orestes dropped to his knees before them, himself too afraid to do or say anything.

After a moment he came to his senses and wordlessly led the men out of the cell, worried that at any minute the spell would be broken and the prisoners would try to escape. He motioned to Koinos and Demetrios to secure the other prisoners.

When the chains in the inner cell had been locked again, the guards began working on the outer cells as well. None of the chains had been damaged in the earthquake. They had all flown loose as if opened by their key.

A quick glance at the candle on the table told Orestes it was about midnight.

As the two guards worked, Orestes stood uncomfortably before the two prisoners. He was still trembling uncontrollably, unable to recover from the chaos of the last few minutes. Death seemed a certainty only a moment before, but now it appeared that everything was okay. What's more, these two prisoners had the chance to simply walk out, but they chose to stay put and rescue *Orestes*, their captor, rather than gain their freedom. Looking at the two prisoners, he carefully considered his next words.

"Sirs, what must I do to be saved?"[269]

"It is as we said before: if you want to be saved, believe in the Lord Jesus."

---

[269] Acts 16:30-31

"Please, I want to hear more about this. Come to my house tonight. I will clean your wounds and give you a meal, only please tell me and everyone else in my house about your message. And please, tell me your name."

"I am Paul. This is Silas."

"Paul, Silas, come with me."

Orestes grabbed their clothes but didn't bother dressing them yet, as this would only exacerbate their open wounds. He gave a few instructions to his guards, who were too bewildered to object, and then led Paul and Silas out of the prison and under the night sky. As they took the short walk to his house, the terror inside of him was slowly replaced with joy. The God that was recognized by Dimnos' girl caused the chains of his prisoners to fly off and yet they stayed put. This God was kind to these servants of his and even kind to Orestes, who knew nothing about him and had never praised him or served him. What's more, this God was *real*; he had actual power over earth and men alike. The promise of these two men was that he could live forever under the protection of a God like that ... it was too good to be true, but then again everything he'd just seen was too impossible for it to be false. What could he possibly have to fear from prisoners, Roman leaders, or any other men if a God like this saw him and knew him and cared about him?

Orestes led the two men into his house.[270] He went around waking up his wife and children and servants. Orders were spoken with excitement and followed with infectious enthusiasm as the servants wondered what their normally serious and reserved master was suddenly so giddy about. One of them was sent to grab a bucket and water, and another set about preparing a meal.

Orestes came back to the entrance to his house where the two men still stood. His wife, having been awoken first, was standing before them. She gave her husband an apprehensive look, no doubt wondering why two nearly naked, bruised, and dirty prisoners were getting dirt and blood on the floor of her house.

"It's okay," he said encouragingly to both his wife and Paul and

---

[270] Acts 16:32-34

Silas. "Come in. Sit. I will clean your wounds."

Paul and Silas entered the house and Orestes brought them to his table just as the water-filled bucket and cloth arrived. Then he set about his task.

He began with Silas. Most of the wounds were on his back with a few more on the chest and legs. The wounds had been sitting too long and he needed to be rougher than he would have hoped to scrub them out. Other than a few grunts and grimaces of pain, the man was quiet while he cleaned the wounds.

Nearly everyone in his household was watching. They still had no idea why they were woken up or why these strange prisoners were here. But they had never seen Orestes behave this way. Even his children were silent as they waited to see what would happen.

When he finished with Silas he moved on to Paul and began the process anew. While he was cleaning Paul's wounds, the meal arrived. He urged the two men to eat, but not before handing them their clothes—brought from the prison—so that they could dress themselves.

Once the two men were dressed, they sat down to eat. A couple of minutes into their meal, his youngest, a teenage boy, let out a yawn and finally spoke up. "Dad, I'm tired. What are we doing?"

"We have to stay awake," said Orestes, "because something very special is happening. These men are going to teach us the most important thing in the world."

This brought questioning expressions from all in the household.

Now addressing everyone, Orestes said, "These two men are named Paul and Silas. They are the ones that Dimnos' girl has been following around for a few days, shouting, 'These men are servants of the Most High God! They are proclaiming to you the way of salvation!' You know about her. She's never been wrong before, not once. And she was right about these men, too. I don't know why, but they ended up in my prison tonight. A city magistrate and a large crowd brought them to me, beaten badly, but they never said what the charge was."

"I saw what happened today," interjected Orestes' wife. "Dimnos and his associates dragged the two men before the city magistrate. They were furious, and they kept saying that the men were teaching 'unlawful customs'. I asked a few people in the gathering crowd, and someone told me that the men had cast the spirit out of the slave girl. She can't tell the future anymore."[271]

Orestes took a moment to process this. "That would make sense then," he said. "Dimnos has gotten very wealthy and has a lot of powerful friends."

Paul and Silas continued eating in silence, neither adding to nor removing from the story.

Orestes spoke again. "The men were brought into our prison and immediately strange things began to happen. As we were bringing them to the inner cell, Paul told us that the salvation the slave girl was talking about was from death itself; that he could show us how to live forever. He said something about God sending his son to save people, first to the Jewish people and then to everyone else. After we locked him and Silas securely with the other prisoners, we left to continue our usual work. They began singing and praying to God, and they didn't stop all evening. They had all of the other prisoners sitting quietly and merely listening to them. And then, a few minutes ago, there was some kind of earthquake. We are nearby the prison here, you must have felt it?"

All he received in reply were baffled expressions. One of his children shook his head, indicating that he hadn't felt an earthquake.

"Immediately after the earthquake the doors to every cell flew open and the chains of every prisoner came off, but nothing was damaged. It was as if they had all somehow been unlocked and removed at exactly the same time. I thought for sure I was going to die!" Orestes carefully left out the detail about the sword. There were hardships to his line of work, but he didn't wish to place them on his family. He continued, "But nothing happened. The prisoners all remained exactly where they were. Paul told me not to worry, that everything was okay. We secured the other prisoners and I immediately brought them here. He's going to tell us all how to be saved!"

The skepticism of a few in the room was overwhelmed by Orestes' enthusiasm. Even his wife couldn't remember a time when he was

---

[271] Acts 16:16-23

more excited. The evidence stacking up in the favor of Paul and Silas was also overwhelming: the prediction from the slave girl who was never wrong, the public driving out of the spirit, the singing and praising God despite their battered bodies, the earthquake, the chains; it was hard to imagine a normal person could have managed all of this.

Paul and Silas finished the last morsels of their meal. Orestes turned a chair to face them and sat in it, waiting expectantly. Everyone else looked intently at the two men.

Paul stood up. He explained to them all about Jesus, starting with the predictions of his coming from the ancient Hebrew texts of the law and the prophets, and then talking about his life and the miracles he performed, his teaching, his death at the hands of the Romans and the Jewish religious leaders, his resurrection, and his instructions after his resurrection to his followers to go and preach his message to the whole world.

Then he told his own story, that he was once a man who had devoted his life to the destruction of those who followed Jesus, but one day Jesus forcibly stopped him, striking him with blindness for three days. But instead of killing him or abusing him in the same way Paul had abused Jesus' followers, he showed him mercy. Paul was given the Holy Spirit and sent to preach Jesus' message to all the peoples outside of Israel who hadn't heard it yet.[272]

"That is why we were put in prison," said Paul. "God is sending us here, to you and to this household, so that every one of you can be saved."

Orestes had never seen anyone speak like these men.

"What do we need to do to be Jesus' followers too?" asked Orestes.

"You must believe in God and in his servant, Jesus. Submit to him as both your king and your savior. Jesus also commands that you be baptized with water so that the Holy Spirit can come upon you and your actions will be a witness to all around you that you belong to him."

Orestes stood up. "Then let me be baptized now! Why wait even until morning? And let everyone in this household who will come with

---

[272] Acts 16:32

me be baptized as well!"

Every member of the household echoed agreement. Within minutes all of them were standing by the riverbank, with nothing but the stars and torchlight to see by. One-by-one, Paul baptized each of them, and then they returned to the house.[273]

Before retiring for the night, Paul told them to meet a woman named Lydia,[274] who could instruct them further and help them meet the other believers in the city.

Orestes prepared a place for them to sleep, and then he and the rest of his household tried to sleep as well, but their excitement was such that few were successful. After only a few hours he woke the men up so they could travel back to the prison before sunrise.

When they arrived at the prison, Orestes told his guards all that had happened. They peppered Paul and Silas with questions. Paul told them the same things he had told Orestes' family the night before. He also told them to go and find the woman Lydia and speak to her to be baptized and learn more.

Shortly after sunrise there was a knock on the outer door. Orestes opened it to see a couple of officers of the magistrates. A minor dread washed over him as he wondered what they could possibly want. It was almost definitely related to Paul and Silas.

"Good morning, Orestes," said one of them. "The magistrates have sent us here concerning those prisoners that were sent here last evening. They want you to let them go."[275]

"Let ... them go?" asked Orestes. "Just like that?"

"Yes," said the man. "Those were their orders. Though, between you and me, if I were those men I'd find some other city in which to go around proselytizing."

"Wait here one moment," said Orestes.

He went over to Paul and Silas and greeted them with a smile. "The magistrates have sent their officers here to tell me to let you two go. You are free!"

Rather than the happy reaction Orestes was expecting, Paul's brow

---

[273] Acts 16:33
[274] Acts 16:14-15, Acts 16:40
[275] Acts 16:35

furrowed and he merely walked by Orestes to the outer door, with Silas following close behind.[276] Orestes trailed after them as they headed outside.

The officers were surprised to see the men produced so quickly, and even more so because they appeared clean and clothed and generally in a much better state than when they were brought in.

Orestes watched as Paul addressed the officers. "They beat us publicly, without a trial, and threw us in prison, even though we are Roman citizens!" At the words "Roman citizens" each of the officers went wide-eyed. "So now do they wish us to leave quietly, and send a message to all the followers of Jesus in this city that they could expect the same treatment? No! Let them come here and publicly escort us out, for everyone to see!"[277]

"You're a Roman citizen?" asked Orestes, baffled.

"Yes," said Paul. "We both are."

"Then why did you not speak up? Why did you not say something before they beat you, or before you were thrown in here, or even afterwards to us? If the Roman government knew you had been treated like this ..."

As he trailed off both he and the officers began to consider just what exactly the Roman government might do. Even the magistrate who sent Paul and Silas to prison may very well end up in prison himself.

Paul turned to him. "Our wounds were for the salvation of you and your household, and we gladly bear them. The reward Jesus offers us far outweighs anything man can do to us." He turned back to the officers. "But, so that you will not harm others as you have harmed us, tell those magistrates to come here, *personally*, and escort us out for everyone to see!"

The officers left nearly at a run. It was not long before the city magistrates arrived to escort Paul and Silas out of the prison.[278] A small crowd had followed them, and others were beginning to gather around, wondering what could be happening that every magistrate in

---

[276] Acts 16:36
[277] Acts 16:37
[278] Acts 16:38-40

The Jailer

the city was suddenly headed to the prison. Orestes and his two guards watched as the party escorted Paul and Silas out in full sight of the crowd, all the while profusely apologizing and pleading with them to forgive the offenses.

As they watched, Demetrios said, "I've seen what Jesus can do, and I can't deny it. Spirits submit to him, chains unlock, doors open, and prisoners are rescued. And he promises even greater things. But ... I've also seen the wounds on the backs of Paul and Silas. They were mocked, beaten, and imprisoned, though they've done nothing wrong. Is it really worth it?"

Orestes turned to the guard and smiled.

"Yes."

Acknowledgements

First, I must thank God, without whom I'm utterly hopeless. In the many years where I have called you my Lord, I have found everything that the Bible says about you to be trustworthy and true: that you are filled with grace and yet also filled with truth, that you are sovereign over all and yet allow us to act individually and independently, that for our benefit and for your name you do not share your glory with false gods, that you care about the whole world and yet you care about me, that I am your special and favored child and so is everyone else because your capacity for love is just that big, that you are just yet filled with mercy, and that you are unstoppably good. Thank you for all that you have done for me.

I also thank my family for supporting (not to mention tolerating) me through the countless hours spent writing, editing, and obsessing about these stories. Thank you to my wife, Charity. Thank you to my four kids: RJ, Devin, Sarah, and Mekhi.

Thank you to those family and friends of mine who have helped me by reading these stories and talking through them. Thank you in particular to my brother, Cliff, who has listened to me drone on about my writing through more meals than I would like to admit.

And thank you, the reader. I hope this has benefitted you in some way. You have no idea how much it means to me that you have taken the time to read these words.

Made in United States
Orlando, FL
28 April 2023